SNATCHED UP BY A HITTA

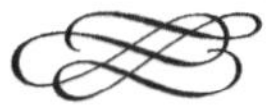

NAI

URBAN AINT DEAD

URBAN AINT DEAD
P.O Box 960780
Riverdale GA., 30296

All rights reserved. Published by URBAN AINT DEAD Publications.

Cover Design: P.Wise/ The Wise Services

Edited By: M.R.Weary

Contact Author on FB: AuthoressNai/ IG: @authoressnai/ TikTok: @authoressnai

Contact Publisher at www.urbanaintdead.com

Email: urbanaintdead@gmail.com

Print ISBN: 979-8-9888415-2-4

CONTENTS

SOUNDTRACKS

Scan the QR Code below to listen to the
Soundtracks/Singles of some of your favorite U.A.D titles:

Don't have Spotify or Apple Music?
No Sweat!

Visit your choice streaming platform and search URBAN AINT DEAD.

Currently on lock serving a bid?
JPay, iHeartRadio, WHATEVER!
We got you covered.

Simply log into your facility's kiosk or tablet, go to music and search URBAN AINT DEAD.

URBAN AINT DEAD

Like & Follow us on social media:
FB - URBAN AINT DEAD
IG: @urbanaintdead
Tik Tok - @urbanaintdead

SUBMISSIONS

Submit the first three chapters of your completed manuscript to <u>urbanaintdead@gmail.com</u>, subject line: Your book's title. The manuscript must be in a .doc file and sent as an attachment. The document should be in Times New Roman, double-spaced, and in size 12 font. Also, provide your synopsis and full contact information. If sending multiple submissions, they must each be in a separate email. Have a story but no way to submit it electronically? You can still submit to URBAN AINT DEAD. Send in the first three chapters, written or typed, of your completed manuscript to:

URBAN AINT DEAD
P.O Box 960780
Riverdale GA., 30296

DO NOT send original manuscript. Must be a duplicate.
Provide your synopsis and a cover letter containing your full contact information.
Thanks for considering URBAN AINT DEAD.

Chapter 1

"Hurry up, Tae. You not moving fast enough." Katori rushed her brother in a hushed tone as they raided the 7-Eleven for the third time this week. It was late and she wanted to get home, but the stop was necessary.

Usually, Dontae was quick, but today his mind was preoccupied, and he couldn't stay focused. Katori picked up on it and at first, she told herself that whatever his issue was he'd better put it aside because business had to be handled, and getting caught was not an option. Seeing that his pace hadn't changed, she took the book bag from him and pulled out a five-dollar bill from her pocket.

"Here," she practically forced the money into his hand, "grab whatever and keep the clerk busy. I can't have you zoned out over here."

"Tori, I'm—."

Katori held her hand up, signaling for her brother to stop speaking. "We'll talk about it when we get outta here. Go head." Shooing him with her hand, she sighed, annoyed that she'd now have to do both of their jobs.

Filling up Tae's book bag and her Coach tote enough to make her content while at the same time not making it obvious that she was raiding the store, Katori made sure to glance up every now and then. Though she had tasked Tae with keeping the clerk busy, she always kept her eyes on everything and everyone. Slick as ever, she proceeded to calmly walk to the front of the store and gestured to Tae that she was making her exit.

Now, had it been any other customer, Katori was almost positive that the clerk would've asked to see her bags. Always prepared with a plan B, she made sure her plan A was clutch. Hence the reason why whenever she was out *five-finger discount* shopping, she dressed the part. With Fall making its debut, she couldn't be as sexy as she normally was, so she had to settle for a pair of tight, True Religion jeans that hugged her hips and made her ass sit up just right. The words FUCK OFF written on the front of her graphic tee that she cut low enough to expose her ample breasts expressed her entire personality. On her feet were a pair of high heeled shoe boots, and she wore a cropped leather jacket to complete the look. She'd long ago realized that her stacked body and attitude allowed her to get over with most men. Danny, the store clerk, was one of them.

"Have a nice day, beautiful," Danny called out as she went to push open the door to exit with Tae not too far behind.

"Yeah, you too, Danny," she responded without bothering to turn around.

Once outside, Katori and Dontae walked across the busy intersection of the Grand Concourse to the bus stop. While they would normally talk after hitting a store, they both waited for the bus in silence. Dontae was still in his head while Katori mentally calculated what she could make off the day's haul. She sold the snacks to the single mothers where she lived for half price, making it so that pocket change was never an issue for her or Tae. She also boosted kids' clothing and would sell those items as well.

Katori wasn't your normal booster, though. Her clientele was strictly single mothers who wanted quality clothing for their kids but couldn't always afford it. Whatever they needed, she made it happen, all while maintaining a full-time job. She was a hustler at heart.

"I still don't get why we hit this 7-Eleven when you know that nigga Danny will give you the stuff for free. Shit, he'll even give you his check just for some conversation," her sixteen-year-old brother let out.

"Well, I ain't selling conversation. And him giving me something would make me indebted to him and we know that's not how I do things." Katori handed Tae his book bag which he threw over his shoulder.

"You mad at me?"

Katori shook her head. "No, I ain't mad. A little annoyed, but not mad."

"Aight," Tae responded and looked away.

The bus pulled up and they boarded. Tae used his school-issued MetroCard and Katori used the same school-issued card, only she'd bought hers off of one of Tae's friends who decided he had better things to do than be tied up in someone's classroom for eight hours. The bus driver gave her a nasty look that she returned before following her brother to the back of the bus with her head held high. Katori wasn't afraid of getting over on any part of the system. The way she saw it, they got over by hiking up the bus fare when they wanted and never keeping the means of transportation up to par.

At 23 years old, most would say that Katori had a chip on her shoulder. Her response to that would be that life had made her the cold bitch she appeared to be. Starting with her being thrown into the position of parent after her mother had died in a house fire three years ago to the day. Katori's mother, Rena, and Tae had been home asleep when a fire broke out in their building. While making sure Tae got out to safety, Rena suffered the brunt of the flames that had accelerated and succumbed to her third-degree burns at the hospital.

That night, Katori had been out at a friend's house when she got the news of her mother's passing. The pain crippled her to the point where she didn't think she'd make it to the hospital, but she knew she had a responsibility to her then thirteen-year-old brother. She'd made it to Dontae in time to flee the hospital before DSS could get a social worker involved. There was no way in hell she'd have her brother be raised by strangers when they had family, or so they thought. The Vincent family had shown her that she and Tae were all they had when no one jumped at the chance to take them in after learning about the tragic loss of their mother.

After the funeral, Katori overheard her aunts going back and forth about who didn't have enough space to accommodate any more people and who couldn't afford it. It was crazy to Katori, seeing as her mother had opened the doors to her three-bedroom apartment plenty of times to different family members in need. Having heard enough of the bullshit, and not one to bite her tongue, Katori made her presence known.

"Y'all ain't gotta worry bout me or Tae. One thing about it and two things for certain, I'm gonna make sure we straight."

Those were the last words she'd spoken to her aunts or any of the family for that matter. Katori never told Tae the real reason they ended up staying with her boyfriend, Rob in his one-bedroom apartment as opposed to one of their aunts' homes. She also didn't let her ill feelings interfere with him having a relationship with their younger cousins. She just kept her distance and lived her life.

"Tori," Tae called her name.

"Hmm?" She answered, without looking up, locked in on a game of Bingo Cash. If there was a way to make some money, she would explore it.

"I gotta talk to you about something." Tae's normal confident tone was filled with uncertainty that Tori picked up on. Putting her phone away in her pocket, she gave him her undivided attention.

"What's wrong?"

Tae took in his surroundings and decided that the semi-crowded bus wasn't the best forum to have the conversation he needed to have with his sister.

"We can talk about it when we get to the crib."

"You know, I really hate when you do that. By the look on your face, I can tell it's serious, so I'll wait this time." Whatever was going on, they'd long ago decided that they'd hold each other down through whatever.

AFTER A FEW STOPS on the bus, an argument with a man standing directly over her, and pushing through a crowd of people who decided to post up near the exit, they finally made it to Rob's apartment. The place they'd called home over the last two years. Katori appreciated him giving them a place to lay their heads, but she'd outgrown both Rob's home and the relationship.

Things weren't the same between Katori and her first love and hadn't been for some time. In the beginning, when she came to him about her and Tae not having anywhere to go, he put a key in her hand without so much of a discussion. He'd developed his own bond with Tae over the years and there was no way he was about to see his girl and her brother out on the street. They moved in and with Katori having a job and her side hustle, she offered to kick in on half the rent, but Rob wouldn't accept it. Knowing how independent his woman was, he proposed that she pay the cable bill and keep the groceries stocked. She agreed and they lived in harmony as a little family for two years.

Things became strained once Tae turned 16. All of a sudden it was, *that lil' nigga eat too much,* or *he gotta play the game all night?* And whatever other complaint Rob could think of. Katori knew what was up though. Rob's real issue was that after many talks about their future, she had decided that she didn't want the baby he so desperately wanted her to carry. For Katori, life was hard as it was taking care of her little brother and making sure the both of them were straight. She knew that bringing a child along for the ride would only add on more to her already full plate. Katori was committed to doing things in excellency and in her mind's eye, if she couldn't give her baby everything life had to offer, including her time, she would rather wait.

So, after many arguments and standing firm on her decision, she saw the changes. Not one to sit on her hands and refusing to live in discord for too long, Katori became distant and went into plot mode. Between working as a receptionist at a dental office and her hustle, she was closer to her savings goal every day.

"I'm gonna hop in the shower and when I get out, be ready to lay all your burdens down, little brother," Katori said, while sticking her key in the door and turning it.

Pushing the door open, an eerie feeling came over her, making her step backward and on Tae's foot, causing him to yell out.

"Damn, Tori! You just gon' step on my—." Tae went silent when a masked gunman turned the corner and pointed a gun directly at Katori's forehead.

"Come in," they heard someone say from a different place in the apartment.

"Close the door," the gunman instructed Tae, who slammed it closed and mugged the guy hard. The gunman returned the look under his mask but silently respected the young kid's

position. Katori took one step so that she was right in front of Tae. Even though the gun had her terrified, she was gonna protect her brother at all costs. "Walk."

She moved slowly and made sure that Tae was right behind her. "We don't—." Katori went to speak, and her words got caught in her throat seeing Rob tied to a chair with his head hanging to his chest. Despite the turn their relationship had taken, Katori wanted to reach out for him, but the fear made her stand still.

"Katori, right?" The same voice that told them to come in spoke and Katori turned her head just as he came into view. The first thing she noticed was his height. He was very tall and his aura exuded confidence. Her eyes then zeroed in on the Louis Vuitton bag in his hand, and her heart dropped knowing that it held her whole $8,000 savings. "It's cool, you don't have to answer. My beef ain't witchu or your brother.

I'm not sure if you know what ya man is into, but he made a move on some territory that I'm sure he knew was off-limits, right Rob."

Rob didn't move, but Katori knew he was alive. From where she stood, she could see his chest rising and falling. As the guy made it in front of him, he lifted Rob's head and Katori could hear Tae whisper, *oh shit,* from behind her. Rob's face was a swollen, bloody mess. Katori surmised that he had gotten into a situation he couldn't talk himself out of this time. She had so many questions, starting with how this man knew about her and most importantly, how did he get his hands on her savings.

Chapter 2

Katori was well aware of how Rob made his money and made no noise about it in the years they'd been together. The money he made selling pounds of weed kept him shelling out thousands to her over the years, dripped in designer, and recently, a roof over her and her brother's heads. In the time he'd been doing his thing, never had his occupation reached the home front until tonight. Wise enough to know that this kind of thing came with the territory, she opted to remain quiet even though she really wanted to let the unwanted visitor know that he had her shit.

"Rob, is this the bag you were talkin' bout?" The man held her bag up in the air. It was hard for Rob to see with one eye swollen shut and the other on its way. "Bossman, you gotta talk to me or I'ma have my boy put a nice size hole in ya head. Is this the bag?"

Katori hoped that he said no, but to her disdain, he gave the opposite answer. "Yea," he let out, his tone low.

The guy opened the bag and pulled out one of the rubber band stacks. He shook his head in disapproval before tossing the money back in the bag and zippering it up. "This is a start. However, judging by the many sales you've made on two of my blocks over the last few months, you, and I both know this ain't gon' cut it. So, what do you propose?" He turned and posed his question to Katori who wore a confused look.

"What do I propose?" Katori reiterated the question.

"Yeah. I mean, this is your bag, right? And I didn't pull that fact from the sky. It has your name engraved on the inside, ma."

Again, Katori went mute. Not because she didn't have anything to say, but because she had put two and two together and she was steaming. Rob knew exactly what he was doing when he told the guy to get that specific bag. He'd somehow known all along that she had money stashed in there. It only put her mind in overdrive, thinking how long he may have known and why he hadn't mentioned it to her.

"The way I see it," the man spoke again, "yo man would rather give up your money, instead of giving access to his. And I don't know how you feel about it, but the shit is pretty fucked up to me. Especially considering the position he holds in the streets as this *real nigga*. Don't seem like a *real nigga* move to me at all. What say you, Tae?"

"Leave my brother out of this," Katori voiced through gritted teeth.

"Respect." The guy put his hand on his chest, apologetically. "Rob, it seems we have ourselves a little issue. See, the last thing I wanna do is take yo girl's money, but at the same time, you know I ain't come see you personally to leave empty-handed." Pulling a gun from his waist, he cocked it back and put it to Rob's temple. "Give me what I came here for and stop wasting my time. I have better shit to do and I'm tryna have a *No Body Count October*. Don't fuck that up for me."

"That's… that's all I…"

"He has a stash in the cushions of the couch," Tae blurted out, making Katori whip her head in his direction. Tae looked past her and at the guy calling the shots. "I helped him put it up, it's in there." He figured his confession would buy them some time and Rob would be grateful for his attempt to save his life.

However, Rob cut his good eye in Tae's direction, seemingly unhappy with his outburst. And if looks could kill, Tae would be a distant memory. Mystery guy tilted his head towards the gunman behind Tae and he pulled out a switchblade. Making his way to the couch, he cut through the cushions. A slice through each one and there the bills were, nestled within the cushion stuffing.

"See how easy shit is when people just cooperate. You

mind grabbing me a bag to put this in, Tae?" The guy requested casually.

"I'll get it," Katori volunteered, locking eyes with Rob who looked like he would break down crying any minute.

"Whatever works for you, love."

Rushing off to the kitchen, Katori reached down under the sink to grab a garbage bag. Standing back up, her hand went for the drawer where they kept the knives and kitchen shears. She put her hand on a butcher knife and something in her told her to look up. When she did, she met the guy's eyes. He shook his head, and she closed the drawer slowly. Heading back into the living room, she handed the bag over and in exchange was given hers.

Relieved that her savings was back in her hands, she went back to where Tae stood and waited for what would happen next. Throwing the last of the bills into the bag, the first gunman nodded to the mystery guy. Without a second thought, he picked up one of the throw pillows to use as a silencer and sent a shot to Rob's head that prompted a shriek from Katori. Tears freely left her eyes as Rob's head dropped forward.

"Let's go."

"Wait, what?! No. We're not going nowhere with your crazy ass."

"Cool. Stay here with the body and let me know how it goes when the police get here and throw him," he pointed to Tae, "in the system."

"You just killed—."

"A snake ass nigga. You can come with me now or get wrapped up in more of his bullshit."

"More? What the hell are you talking about?!" Katori raised her voice.

"I'll explain in the car," was the only response she was given. "Wipe down everything we came in contact with then make it look like a robbery," he said to his counterpart before walking past Katori and Tae. "You don't have long to decide. I'm parked across the street, in the Prius. I won't be there for long."

KATORI HEARD the front door close as her eyes lingered on Rob's motionless body a few seconds longer. The mystery man's counterpart seemed oblivious to the whole scene as he moved around Katori and Tae, trashing the place. Feeling her arm being tugged on, she averted her gaze.

"We gotta get outta here, Tori," Tae expressed with urgency. Seeing Rob get knocked off right in front of him messed his head up, but even at his young age, he knew the magnitude of the situation if they were to stick around any longer. Tae couldn't bear the thought of being separated from his sister. Especially not with the recent turn of events in his life that he'd yet to divulge to her.

"Grab what you can and put it in your duffle bag. I'll figure out the rest," Katori said with her feet still planted.

"I ain't moving till you move," Tae let her know, matter of factly.

Sighing, Katori took Tae's hand and stepped over the overturned coffee table.

"Y'all got ten minutes," the accomplice alerted the two. There was no time to really pack anything but their necessities. Given the severity of the situation, they'd have to figure everything else out as they went along.

As Katori rushed to pack, she thought about the last conversation she had with Rob. It was heated and they'd exchanged a few choice words that she felt there was no coming back from.

"I don't know what the fuck you mad about, I ain't saying shit that ain't true," Rob argued while lighting his kush-filled blunt.

"That's the thing, every time I become quiet you take it as me being mad when I'm really just processing." Katori wasn't quick to speak when in disagreement, especially when it was about a sensitive topic. She had realized from the start of the conversation that it wouldn't end well.

"Yeah, processing another bullshit ass excuse to give me as to why you don't wanna carry my seed," Rob spat. "That's what you were put on this earth to do. And don't give me no bullshit excuse about taking care of Tae either. That lil nigga is a grown-ass man."

Katori examined her French manicure and shook her head. "If you think talkin' to me crazy is going to convince me to want a baby, you got another thing coming."

"After all this time, Tori. Me putting a roof over...you know

what, fuck it." Taking a pull of the weed, he let it settle in his lungs before exhaling.

Although Katori was offended that he'd mentioned opening his doors for her and Tae, she wouldn't admit it out loud.

"Lemme ask you a question, Rob. Did you let me and Tae move in here just so you could hold some shit over my head?"

Again, he inhaled and then exhaled, blowing smoke in her direction. "What kinda lame as shit is that to do?"

Katori shrugged. "I don't know. It's starting to seem that way, though. Understand this, if I ever gave you the impression that I needed you to be my savior, that was my bad. I wanna make it clear right here, right now that me giving you a baby will not be a reward for your good deed. I wasn't ready when you first brought it up and I'm not ready now."

"Heard you. You won't hear shit else about it. Just remember, what you won't do, the next woman will." His voice was laced with disdain that Katori made note of.

The interaction further solidified the ending of the relationship.

"You ready?" Katori asked Tae as she walked out into the hallway with what she could fit in her Louie luggage and the knapsack that held her savings. She'd traded her heels for a pair of New Balance to move around better.

"Yeah, just grabbing this picture of mommy." Tae grabbed the framed picture of their mother from the closet where he kept his belongings and put it in his bag.

Heading back to the front of the house, the once organized living room, courtesy of Katori's love for cleaning was now in complete disarray. Rob's body was still in the same position. With the scene already etched in her brain, Katori didn't take another look as she and Tae made their way to the front door.

"Don't touch the doorknob with your hands," the accomplice said to them.

She wanted to say something smart in response, but let it go. Tae stepped around her and used the sleeve on his hoodie to open the door. It was a good thing that Rob lived in a building where people stayed to themselves and minded their business for the most part. While sometimes it was a blessing, it was a curse when someone really needed help. Glancing to the left and right, Katori waved for Tae to come out. She wanted to do her best to avoid being seen leaving the apartment.

They decided to take the steps down to the lobby. Leaving the building, she spotted the Prius immediately. The mystery guy had kept his word by waiting on them. It was the one thing that kept her moving towards the car and not making a detour up the block.

"You sure about this?" Tae asked his sister, undoubtedly leery about the situation at hand as he walked beside her.

"No," she answered honestly. "The only thing I'm sure of is that I'll never let anything bad happen to us," Katori spoke with conviction and Tae nodded, already knowing how his sister was coming about him. And she meant every word, even though it seemed morally wrong.

As they got closer to the Prius, Katori went around the

back of it and snapped a picture of the license plate. Although she was blindly going with the mystery man, she would make sure to get the license plate info over to her best friend. Opening the back passenger door, they were halted by the guy's voice.

"I ain't no Uber, ma. One of y'all sit up front," he stated.

"Can you pop the trunk?" Katori requested, ignoring his statement. The trunk opened and she and Tae tossed their heavier bags inside. Tae got in the backseat while she slid in the passenger, clutching her savings. "Look, I don't know what you got going on or even what you have planned for us but know that I'm not gonna make it easy for you if it comes down to it."

The mystery guy gave Katori a full once over with his dark brown eyes. She felt uncomfortable under his stare. It was like he was searching for something, and she didn't like it. His stare made her feel vulnerable.

"I don't have any intention of hurting you or your brother if that's what you're getting at. You'll understand why what happened back there was necessary soon enough." He started up the car and pulled off.

How he'd justify killing Rob was questionable to Katori. She knew something was up and she couldn't shake the feeling that leaving with this man was sure to open up Pandora's Box.

Chapter 3

"This the nigga that's been talkin' to Detective Ryan and opened up the two shops on two of our... I mean your blocks." Trill showed his boy the pictures he'd taken of Rob, the weed man during one of his many morning meetings at a diner out in Queens.

East picked up the photos, carefully examining and dissecting even the smallest details that the untrained eye would miss. This wasn't news to him. Not only had he heard the name Rob prior to the stunt he pulled, but he also had Detective Ryan on his payroll. He was aware of the dry snitching after the first meet up. Rob had made a name for himself as a man to see for all kinds of weed and while he had his clientele, he wanted more. And it was cool to want to expand, but to step on another man's toes, a man who had the power to cut your lights off was just stupid.

What had East hot wasn't just that Rob was snitching to get rid *of the competition, but he'd started to try his hand in the coke game. A game that East had sewed up in specific spots throughout the New York City area. As opposed to getting on the right way, Rob wanted to take over and figured the only way to do so was by talking to the police. Only he'd confided in the wrong person and had written a check that his ass couldn't cash. That said, East practically gave Rob the rope to hang himself by giving him the space to open up shop all while collecting information from Detective Ryan and now Trill.*

"Good work, Trill. I'll handle everything else from here. You get the information on his girl like I asked?"

"You know I'm thorough with my shit, East. But check this, shorty ain't even his main girl. Mind you, the one you had me look up is the one that stay with him. The other one is his baby mama. Nigga be over there daily. Shorty that stays with him prolly don't even know the half." Trill handed him a manilla folder.

"Preciate you. The man got a lot going on, huh?"

"Shiidd, more than a little bit if you ask me. I mean, it ain't uncommon for niggas to be out here doing they one, two, but I ain't hiding no baby. That's next level fuck shit."

East nodded in agreement. Reaching into his desk drawer, he pulled out two thick envelopes. One was labeled DT and the other with Trill's name. "I need you to deliver that to Detective Ryan for me and let him know to cancel any further meetings with Rob."

"I got you. Same place?" Trill asked, hoping East had changed the location of their old meet up spot. East smirked and nodded. "Damn, man, y'all gotta pick a better meet up spot than the cemetery. It's midnight."

"Hey," East shrugged, "consider it paying your respects to the dead. You know we got a few bodies in there."

Trill was once East's partner in the game. They had come up together, with East being the brains and Trill being the muscle. The two were like night and day, with Trill being the hot headed one.

His hot-headed ways kept niggas off their blocks and their team in line. Both East and Trill ruled with iron fists, but East knew when to turn down his gangsta while Trill woke up and went to sleep on timing. It was what got him into trouble with the law often and East bailing him out. His last run in made him step away from the game altogether. Trill got caught up on an illegal gun charge and unlike the other times, East couldn't pay his boy out of having to answer to it.

He was sentenced to five years on the charge and on the same day of his sentencing, his girl committed suicide. When he found out the love of his life had taken her own, it messed his head up bad. Not being able to grieve and mourn her loss properly made it even worse. Being behind the wall there was no space for grief. Tears made you appear weak, so in the five years that he was down, Trill didn't shed any.

He'd blamed himself then and still blamed himself till this day for Shante killing herself. At first, he was angry that she chose to go out that way, but the time he spent sitting made him see that his other half was carrying some kind of pain that he couldn't see, hear, or feel. All Trill saw was his rider as she appeared at every court date and made sure to answer every call. When he was released, he let East know that he needed to step down from his position because being in the game only reminded him of the times, she begged him to get out and make legal money. Shante came from a good home and like most good girls, she found Trill's bad boy swag attractive. The only difference was, she didn't try to fit into his world nor bring him into hers. She did, however, want him to leave the game knowing there was no retirement plan once he reached a certain age.

Trill would always brush her off and tell her he was made for the game. All the talking and encouragement in the world wouldn't make him step down from his post. But her death...her death made him see things clearer and the fact that he couldn't be there to stop it, made him want to honor her by hanging the street shit up. East couldn't have predicted that Trill would become the hood P.I. The people that who once worked under Trill thought that he was crazy for leaving the game, but they dared not utter their objection. Either way, East respected Trill's decision and would use his services often when he needed information.

"Man, that was then, this is now," Trill said. "I ain't gon' lie though, seeing that nigga Rob on that snake shit made me wanna hop back in the passenger seat just to get at his ass. You know I take that snitchin' shit to heart."

East didn't get his hopes up nor did he encourage Trill's thoughts. "Nah, one of us gotta remain legit somehow. You were just telling me about taking this P.I. shit to the next level. Keep going, bruh."

"Nigga, if this ain't legit I don't know what is. We're holding a meeting at your coffee shop. I mean, yeah, it's late as hell but what somebody gon' say about you being in your establishment after hours? And what nigga in the game you know got a coffee shop?"

East looked around his quaint office and couldn't help but to let out a chuckle. Out of all of the businesses he could've purchased to funnel his money through, who knew that a coffee shop in the middle of Midtown Manhattan would be it. He'd even gone as far as to hire an all-white staff just to keep up appearances. The manager, though, was his aunt Boo and she was as black as they came. Aunt Boo kept the place moving and the staff loved her. East loved that she was herself, too; unapologetically black for her full shift.

"Yeah, I guess you're right. Still, I need you to keep up your work unless you're ready to dive back into this shit 100%. You know ain't no one foot in, one foot out in this business."

"Yeah, I know." Trill paused and thought for a brief moment before holding his fist out for East to dap. "Lemme get up outta here, bro. Let the boy know I'm on my way and don't be late."

"Already on it. Keep your head up, Trill." They dapped it up and Trill left, leaving East alone with his thoughts and the visuals of Katori Vincent.

East glanced over at Katori as he drove and picked up on how tight she held her bag and blinked multiple times, indicating that she was fighting her sleep. It was clear to him that she refused to lose the battle to rest. Neither of them had spoken during the forty-minute drive. East had purposely kept the radio off and all that could be heard were the sounds of the road and the clicking sound every time he signaled to switch lanes. Tae had fallen asleep in the back seat, his tall frame doing its best to get comfortable just as East had in the front seat of the small car.

"How much longer until we get to where you're taking us?" Katori finally spoke. Her voice was filled with irritation.

Her pictures do her no justice, East thought to himself. Katori was a beautiful, chocolate woman with high cheekbones, plump lips, and round dough-shaped eyes. She wore her hair in a braided style that she had up in a bun that sat up on her head, giving East a full look at her small ears and delicate neck. He could tell her skin was soft and moisturized just from the looks of it. East hadn't really checked out her body up close but by the way, her hips filled the passenger seat, he knew she had just the right amount of thickness.

She was attractive and something in East figured she knew that, but her attitude made her unapproachable. He then thought about the other pictures that Trill had in the manilla envelope he'd given him of Rob's baby mother. She was a pretty girl, too. She resembled Katori in thickness, likely from bearing a child, but she wasn't Katori. Katori had a glow to her beauty. One that she couldn't hide behind her tough exterior.

"Hello, did you hear what I said?" She pushed, waving her hand in his direction.

"Yeah, we're pulling up in a minute."

"And where are we pulling up to?"

"Somewhere for the two of you to lay low for a week or two. The hood usually stops asking questions after a few days.:

Katori scoffed. "This shit is absolutely insane. I don't need these kinds of problems."

"Why you think I'm offering you a way around this shit?" East could've told her that he knew all about her and her brother as far as their family background was concerned. He was detailed in his request when he put Trill on the job of looking into what all Katori had going on. Ultimately, it helped determine whether or not she'd have to meet the same fate as Rob if she had anything to do with his street dealings.

"I don't know what you're offering. What I do know is that in a matter of minutes, you've come in and disrupted my life. Like, literally turned my shit upside down without any warning. Quite frankly, the only two reasons I'm in this car right now is because of my brother and the fact that you kept it solid and waited for us. And no, I don't have a thank you in me because the fact still remains that you just killed a man that I had love for. I gotta live with that shit every day going forward." Katori pointed to her chest for emphasis. Tears burned her eyes, and she had a scream stuck in her throat that she wanted so badly to let go of but couldn't. She wanted to remain a stranger to raw emotion, and she didn't want to alarm Tae who was still asleep in the backseat. "So, excuse me if I'm not in the headspace to jump for gratitude at the moment."

"Didn't know you cared about that nigga like that." East found himself shaking his head internally at her grief. He was sure that if she knew about her man fucking around and having a kid, her hurt would be different.

"You don't know me to know what I care about," Katori

countered. "And had you known, would it have stopped you from killing him?"

The car came to a stop and East put it in park. He looked her dead in her face and kept it 100. "No. And you may find that fucked up, but this is life and in life people make choices. Rob made a choice to take from me and then doubled down by talking to the police about some shit he knew nothing about. Niggas like that need to be eradicated so that they don't groom more like them. Be thankful that you didn't procreate with him. A nigga ain't lookin' for no appreciation party either, shorty. We're here."

Opening the driver's side door, East hopped out of the car, leaving Katori to reflect on what he'd said. He didn't mean to come off harsh, but it was imperative for her to know that he didn't offer her and Tae an out as a way to clean his face with her for killing Rob. It was strictly to keep the both of them safe, at least that's what he told himself. He didn't quite understand where his need to protect her came from and he was sure that no one else would either. It wouldn't stop him from doing what he'd set out to do though. He knocked on the back passenger window that Tae had rested his head against, prompting him to spring up with his fist in the air.

"That's what I'm talkin' bout, always be on timing," East encouraged. He put his fist up against the window and Tae nodded. "Y'all can come out."

"Come on, Tae," Katori said, and he complied, opening his

door. Getting out of the car, Katori went around back to the trunk.

"Y'all need help with anything?" East inquired, popping the trunk.

"We got it," Katori spoke for both of them, pulling out her suitcase and handing Tae his duffle bag. East nodded and stepped back onto the sidewalk. "You don't have to talk to him, Tae. Soon as I figure out some shit and everything dies down, we outta here." Pulling her suitcase along, they followed East to the building.

It was a luxury high-rise with a doorman who stood outside. He didn't seem like your average doorman, though. More like hired security. Dressed in a suit, the man was lean, and his straight face let you know that he didn't take no shit. His jawline was tight, not a smile or smirk in sight.

"Evening, Mr. E." He greeted East.

"Wassup, Paul. These are my guests, Katori and Dontae." Hearing the mystery guy say her name again and now Tae's full name had Katori feeling crazy for not having asked his after being in a car with him for almost an hour. "They'll be here for a lil' bit, so I expect that they'll have no issues in their comings and goings."

"None at all, Mr. E. I'll see to it that they have no issues during their stay." Although the doorman toward over East by a foot, the respect that he showed couldn't be missed. Both Katori and Tae had picked up on it.

The doorman held the door open for the trio to walk through and they headed for the elevators. Katori took in the marble floors and expensive paintings along the walls in the lobby. She could only imagine what the mystery man's place looked like. She secretly marveled. The elevator door dinged, and the doors opened. An elderly white couple walked out, making sure to give the group a disapproving stare as they exited.

"Problem?" Katori taunted. The wrinkle-faced Karen and Ken scurried along.

East snickered and held the elevator door open with one hand and signaled her along with the other. "Come on for you have them people report me, shorty. It's hard enough being one of the few black people in this overpriced ass building."

Rolling her eyes, Katori stepped onto the elevator and stood off in the corner opposite of East. Even with her face turned up in the same frown she'd had since he met her, she was still pretty as hell. East openly admired her, not bothering to avert his eyes when she caught him staring. In fact, he challenged her by turning so that she was in his direct eyesight. The elevator dinged and Katori stepped off first and began walking as if she knew where she was going.

"You been here before?" East questioned, jokingly. He stopped in front of his door, and punched a few numbers into a keypad, unlocking his condo.

Katori was embarrassed that she had walked past the door but doubled back with her head held up high and entered behind Tae.

"Oooouu, wee, this shit—." Katori shook her head at him,

giving him the cue to tone down his excitement. She didn't need the mystery guy thinking they had never been in a nice apartment. In her head, he already felt like he was saving them.

"Preciate it, kidd," East let out. "Y'all have access to everything. I'm barely here so the groceries may be light. I ain't gon lie it's prolly just a whole bunch of water, fruit, and juice in the fridge. I can order some shit on Instacart real quick and have it delivered." He took out his phone to pull up the app.

"We're good," Katori spoke. "I can figure that out for us."

"Aight, cool." East knew she already had her guard up and he didn't wanna force anything on her. "Linen closet is here with fresh towels, washcloths, and all that." He opened up a closet that was across from the kitchen to show them. "The main bathroom is around the corner and to your left. There are two bedrooms that each have a bathroom in them. Both beds have fresh sheets and blankets on them. I gotta handle some shit. The code to the door is 0627. Y'all try to have a good night, I know today was a lot."

East went to leave out the door and Katori looked over at Tae who shrugged his shoulders and went to give himself a tour of the condo. A thought popped into Katori's head, making her dart over to the front door to catch East.

"Hey," she called out just as he stepped onto the elevator. He held the door open and peeked his head out. "What is your name?"

"Eastland."

"Eastland?" She repeated, thinking the name was odd but unique.

"I know. My momma was drunk off the yak when she named me and my sister. You can call me East."

"Alright."

"Goodnight, Katori." Katori didn't respond. She closed the door behind her and leaned up against it. She didn't know what would come of the morning, but she could bet that sleep wouldn't come easy.

Chapter 4

Katori tossed and turned all night, unable to get a wink of sleep as images of Rob's body slumped over in his chair flooded her mind. She half expected for her phone to be full of calls and text messages from people asking where she was and if she knew what happened to him, but the only text she had was from her best friend, Fatima asking if she was okay. Katori didn't have it in her to even pick up the phone and call her R.O.D. She knew if she did, Fatima would know something was wrong immediately. They knew each other inside and out.

It was likely the reason why Fatima hadn't called once she saw that Katori hadn't responded. Fatima knew that her best friend went through her bouts with depression and sometimes needed a day to decompress at any given time. She never let it go past a day, though, so Katori expected her phone to ring soon. Tears drenched the silk pillowcase she lay on, in the most comfortable bed she'd ever slept in. The plush duvet that covered her body did nothing to aid in her restlessness or ease the guilt she felt. While it wasn't her fault that Rob was dead, she couldn't shake the feeling. He was gone and there was nothing she nor anyone else could've done to change his fate according to East. She'd replayed what he'd revealed to her in the car about Rob's street dealings and still concluded that it didn't warrant his death.

Katori would have been able to sleep at night had he been robbed or even beat up. But death…death was too final for her. Familiar with the code of the streets, she had to accept that the old saying, *you reap what you sow*, was alive and well. Tossing for the umpteenth time, her body told her to get up. Getting out of bed, she picked up her phone and stood to her feet. Remembering the tour she and Tae had taken of the place once East had left, she maneuvered through the darkness to get to the kitchen. Making a right, she heard Tae's voice. He spoke in a hushed tone, but in the stillness of the condo, she could hear both him and another voice she assumed was on the phone clearly.

"**So, what you gon' do?**" Tae questioned whomever he was speaking to.

"**I don't know, Dontae. We just found out two days ago.**" Katori recognized the voice of Tae's girlfriend, Kita.

"**I know, Kita, but the longer we wait to decide what we're gonna do, the more difficult this shit becomes.**"

"**Don't you think I know that Tae. I can't make this**

decision alone. Did you get a chance to talk to your sister yet?" Kita was stressing the same as Tae, if not more. Both were scared to make a decision that would undoubtedly change the course of both of their young lives.

Tae sighed and ran his hand down his face. "No, I haven't gotten a chance to. And you're not alone, Kita. We're gonna make a decision together. Remember, we both played a part." Katori wanted to intercept their conversation, but from what she'd heard so far, she figured it would be best to hear it in full.

"Alright. Try to talk to her today, please. You know I don't have anybody here to help me out. I know your sister is going to be pissed. She gon' call me all types of names."

"No, she not, Kita. If anything, she gon' kick my ass. Either way, we gon' figure it out and soon, aight."

"Okay," Kita responded in a low tone and sniffled.

"Shit, don't cry, man. I got you. And remember what I said, don't tell anybody shit. Especially not your bum ass friends." Tae may have been harsh in his delivery, but he was always like that when it came to the circle Kita hung with.

"You always call them bums when I'm the one who used to wear hand-me-downs until we became a couple."

"Yeah, well, you're pretty and you're a good person. Fly shit don't make you. Them bum ass bitches you call friends just feed off your good energy and don't got or want nothing. Keep them out of our business."

"I hear you, Tae. Let me go get some more sleep before school. I love you, okay."

"I love you, too, bae. I'll see you later." As soon as the conversation was over, Katori made her presence known by flicking on the light. Tae didn't acknowledge her presence at first. His burden was too heavy to even lift his head.

Sliding out the chair next to him at the kitchen island, Katori pulled her brother to her and held him close. "Whatever it is, I ain't gon love you no less, Tae. Whatever it is, we gon get through that shit together. We gon get through all this shit together."

"Kita, pregnant," Tae finally spit out while pulling away from her embrace.

Katori wasn't prepared for his admission. She couldn't even comprehend what he'd just said but dared not to ask him to repeat it. She wasn't naïve to think that her handsome, advanced little brother wasn't hunching on his girlfriend but getting someone pregnant at 16 years old was far beyond what she expected.

"Tae, really? Pregnant, man."

"I know, Tori. It was one slip up. I fucked up, I mean messed up bad."

"Shit, you might as well cuss. You out here having sex raw." Unable to control her hand, she brought it up and across his head.

"Ouch, what the hell Tori!" Had he not had a head full of soft curls, he would've really felt the sting of the slap. "Come on, man."

"Come on man, my ass. Y'all too young to be out here being so reckless and careless. And you know that girl situation. The last thing she needs is a baby. Her people don't even give a fuck about her enough to make sure she straight. And you know I'm not saying this to be mean because I genuinely adore her, and I hate the circumstances she gotta live under."

Kita lived in a dysfunctional household with her aunt who had custody of her and two cousins who were jealous of her. It was clear that whatever hate her cousins had for her had something to do with how her aunt felt about her mother, and unfortunately, Kita had to deal with it. She often found solace with Tae and Katori. Even though they didn't have a place of their own, hanging with Tae at Rob's house was a regular occurrence for Kita and she appreciated the escape.

"I know that, too. I need you to talk to her cause I already know what my decision is, and I don't wanna come off as insensitive. I'd love for Kita to be the mother of my children one day. Right now, we aren't even in a position to take care of ourselves, let alone a baby. And now we're on the run."

"Whoa," Katori put her hand up, "first off, we ain't on the run cause we ain't do shit. We're just staying out the way to avoid being thrust into some bullshit we had nothing to do with. We're still going about life as normal. No boosting until further notice, though. This pregnancy thing…" Katori sighed and shook her head. "You really threw me for a loop with this one. And although I really wanna beat you like somebody out in the street right now, I know it won't undo what's already been done. I'll have a conversation with Kita to see where her head is. Shit, y'all couldn't have picked a better time to spring this on me. You know I love Kita like a little sister, but you," she pointed to him, "are my responsibility. Know that I have your best interest at heart always. I'm telling you this because I don't want you to think that my conversation with her will feature some kind of fairytale."

Tae was aware that his sister was gonna give it to Kita straight with no chaser. And while he knew it would be hard for her to fully digest at first, the conversation was needed. He believed that Kita knew it as well, which is why she was pushing so hard for him to tell Katori.

"I understand and she does, too."

"Good." Catching the time on the refrigerator, Katori decided to head back to bed and encouraged Tae to do the same. She didn't want him to miss a day of school.

"I love you, sis," Tae said while standing at the entryway to the bedroom he was occupying.

"I love you, too, Tae. You know I mean it when I say I got us, right." Katori needed to ensure that he not only knew that, but he believed it.

"Never once doubted you. Goodnight."

His confidence in her made her smile a little. "Night." Climbing back in the bed, Katori sent a text back to her best friend, letting her know she was okay, then navigated to her Apple music store. Selecting her sleep playlist, she turned her volume up, and let the sounds of the rain sing her a lullaby.

KATORI'S ALARM went off at its normal scheduled time and she rolled over in the bed. Like clockwork, she awoke at 6 a.m. daily and was out of the house by seven. She'd already prepared to be late to work and for Tae to receive his first tardy. According to her maps, East had them out in Westchester and she had to figure out how to navigate without Ubers eating her pockets up. Stretching, she got out of the bed, walked around to the front of it, and checked her phone. She had two missed calls and a voicemail, both from Rob's sister, Patrice. Katori and Patrice were cordial off the strength of Rob, but she could do without ever speaking to her.

Patrice was a jealous wench and often gave off the vibe like she wanted to be with her brother. It was weird to Katori, but Rob was quick to let her know that just as protective as she was over Tae, Patrice was about him. Still, Katori didn't buy it and kept their interactions to a minimum. She dreaded calling her back but knew she had to. Swiping up to unlock her phone, she pressed Patrice's name to call. The call connected on the first ring.

"Hello," Patrice spoke and Katori could tell she'd been crying, maybe even yelling at some point because of the hoarseness in her voice.

"You called?"

"Yeah," Patrice sniffled. "They... they... they found Rob's

body in his apartment this morning. Somebody killed my brother."

"Whatttt?!" Katori exclaimed. She shocked herself with her reaction.

"Yes, early this morning. The landlord went in to fix something and found him. I don't know what to do. I know y 'all weren't together, but I thought you should know."

Patrice's statement made Katori's lip twist up in confusion. Instead of disputing what was said and telling her the real, she figured she'd use it to her advantage. Though it sounded fucked up, Katori wanted to ensure that she and Tae weren't associated with what had happened only hours ago. That said, she went along with Patrice's perception of what her relationship was.

"Damn, Rob. I can't believe this shit."

"He didn't fuck with nobody, Katori. You know my brother made his money, loved his people, and stayed out the way. And now my nephew gotta grow—." Patrice paused and the line went silent, giving Katori a few seconds to digest what she'd just revealed.

"What did you just say?"

"I... I'm sorry. Now is not the time to talk about that."

Katori's first thought was to say something disrespectful, but she knew she had to tread lightly due to the situation. But what she wasn't going to do was let the comment just float in the air. "You're right. Now is not the time to speak on the fact that your brother had a secret baby on me. So, before I get to speaking ill of the dead, I'ma let you go. Again, I'm sorry for your loss." Katori hit the end button on her phone and went to block Patrice's number but stopped herself. Something told her she'd want to have it at some point.

"Tori," Tae called out her name.

"Yeah," she responded, phone still in hand, fully letting the news of Rob's secret baby settle in. She let out an involuntary chuckle at the shock of it all. It was the only thing she could do to keep from tweaking out.

"You know what time we gon' be heading out?" Tae entered the room she occupied, shirtless with a towel around his waist. From the wet curls, she knew he'd just showered.

"Why are you walking around another man's crib with a towel on and your chest out, Dontae? This ain't our shit, go put some clothes on!" Her statement came out rougher than she intended, causing Tae's brow to rise.

"What happened? Somebody call you bout Rob?" Tae questioned, spot on. He wasn't easily offended when it came to his sister. He knew when Katori was snapping because she was mad and when she had something on her mind.

"Yeah. I just got off the phone with Patrice. The landlord found his body."

Turning, she reached for her bag on the ottoman and looked through it to find something to wear. She planned to stop by Fatima's house to change into her work clothes before her shift. It wasn't uncommon for her to leave a few outfits at her house in the event she spent the night or there was an emergency. It helped that Fatima lived a couple blocks from her job.

"Damn," Tae let out, "so what does that mean for us?"

"You let me worry bout that. You have enough problems as it is. Go get ready. I'm gonna check to see what's in the fridge to whip up for breakfast after I shower and get dressed."

"Aight. I saw some eggs and cheese in there. I'd imagine he'd have bread."

"Okay, cool."

Tae made his exit, leaving Katori the space to get her mind right and prepare for the day. While setting the shower, her mind couldn't help but to wonder about the signs she missed with Rob. It further confirmed how out of touch she'd become in the relationship. Had they been in a good space there was no way he would've been able to have a baby right under her nose, let alone carry on another relationship. Getting into the shower, she prepared to wash her body and let any feelings she had for Rob go down the drain.

Katori had no problem detaching once she was done wrong. In fact, a part of her was glad she didn't have to face Rob with what she'd found out. With her volatile temper, there was no telling how it would've gone down. Pressed for time, she washed her body with the body wash that was in the shower caddy, rinsed off, and stepped out onto the fluffy bath rug. Her mind was so consumed with her thoughts that she didn't hear her phone ringing until it stopped. She also didn't notice that in her haste to get ready, she'd forgotten to grab a towel.

"Shit," she cussed out loud, thinking about the trek of

water she was sure to leave as she walked over to her phone. Searching for a quick solution, she looked over at the decorative towels that hung up on the rack and decided to use one to pat her body dry. Normally, she wouldn't be so trifling, but she reasoned it would be better than having to clean the water up from the floor.

Walking out of the bathroom naked, Katori tiptoed across the carpeted floor. Picking up her phone to see who the missed call was from; an incoming call came in again from the same number. She didn't recognize it but figured if the caller dialed her number again, they clearly knew who they were dialing and wanted to talk.

"Hello?"

"**Good morning, what time do you have to be at work? And what time does your brother have to be at school?**" Katori moved the phone from her ear, picking up East's voice. Why she'd committed it to memory in the first place was a mystery to her. Even more of a mystery than how he'd gotten her number. "**Hello?**"

"**Ummm I'm not sure why that's your business. How'd you even get my number? And how do you know that I have a job to get to?**"

"**You don't seem like the slouch type, and I know y'all gon' need a ride. All that other shit about the how is irrelevant. Time?**"

Thinking that she needed to save every dime she had, she decided to take him up on the offer. "**We'll be downstairs by 7:15.**"

"**Cool. I'll let my people know.**"

"**Your people?**" Katori repeated, face screwed up. "**I didn't agree to you pawning us off on one of your cronies.**"

"**My what?**" He chuckled. "**What the fuck is a crony, shorty?**"

Sucking her teeth, Katori shook her head. "**Don't worry bout it. We'll get an Uber.**"

"**Aight. I got some shit to handle. My people will be downstairs by 7:10.**" East completely ignored her statement.

"**Well, he'll just be sitting out there.**"

"**Man, enjoy your day, shorty. It's too early to be all mean and shit. Wait till the Winter hit, then you can act all cold.**"

"**Yeah, okay.**" Ending the call, she went to her texts and sent her supervisor a message to let him know she'd be an hour late at the most. Dropping her phone on the bed, she quickly lotioned her body and put her clothes on. Heading back to the bathroom, she searched under the sink for cleaning supplies. She wanted the bathroom to look the same way it had before she used it.

Once fully put together for the day, she picked up her bag with her savings and tossed her phone and keys inside her purse. Taking note of the time on the clock that hung on the wall, Katori reasoned that making breakfast would make them later than she wanted to be.

"Tae, I'm not gonna have time to make breakfast. We can stop at a Starbucks or Dunkin on our way." Walking out of the room, Katori realized she didn't have a key to lock up the condo and had forgotten the code. "Dammit, now I gotta call him back," she said out loud to herself.

"That's cool," Tae said, coming out of the room fully dressed with his Sprayground bookbag on his shoulder. "You requested the Uber yet? I told Kita to let our homeroom teacher know I'm gonna be late due to a family emergency."

"Cool. You need me to write you a note or something?"

"I'm grown, Tori. I ain't in third grade."

"Yeah, okay. Being grown got your ass growing gray hairs about your little slip up." Tae went silent. "Too soon?"

"Nah, right on time. I need the reminder so that I never slip up again."

"That's a fact. Gimme a second to order the Uber."

"I'ma grab a bottle of water."

Opening her phone, Katori hit the green phone symbol to get to her recent calls. She tapped the last call and East answered on the second ring.

"Wassup, girl."

"How am I supposed to lock the door?"

"It'll automatically lock when you leave. I figured you'd forget the code. I'll text it to your phone, so you have it to get back in."

"Okay."

"Ay," East stopped her before she could hang up, **"I get that you don't wanna be friendly with a nigga and all, but don't hang up on me again. That shit rude and it's one of my pet peeves. I'm big on respect. You respect me, I respect you. You disrespect me and..."**

"**Yeah, I get it,**" she cut him off. "**I need to order my Uber, so I'm gonna hang up now.**" She was sarcastic in her response but had taken in what he said and didn't hang up.

"**No, you not. I'm waiting on y 'all out front. See you in a minute. Now, you can hang up.**" He was first to clear the line, leaving her stuck once again.

"Ready?"

"Yeah, let's go."

They both headed for the door, Katori hesitant about being in East's presence again. *I don't know what he wants but this ain't it,* she thought to herself as she closed the door to the condo. She needed to get to her best friend. Fatima was the only person Katori could be vulnerable with outside of her brother. And right now, the counselor needed counseling.

Chapter 5

Getting off the elevator, in the lobby, Katori and Tae spotted the stern-faced doorman from the previous night. His eyes were trained on the street, and he looked up just as they got closer.

"Good morning," he spoke. Judging by his outward demeanor, Katori didn't expect a greeting.

"Morning," both Tori and Tae said at the same time.

"Your ride is outside. Should either of you need anything during your stay, don't hesitate to reach out."

"Thank you," Katori spoke, politely.

Nodding, he pushed the door open for them to exit. Katori searched the street, expecting to find the Prius they'd rode in the night before, only it wasn't there. The beeping of a horn caught her attention. East rolled down the window of a Black Audi and signaled them over to the car with a nod of his head. Katori glanced over at Tae, who awaited her signal for their next move.

"Come on," she finally instructed. Finding herself headed to the backseat along with Tae, she was stopped by the beeping of East's horn.

"Shorty, we discussed that. This ain't no Uber. Get yo pretty ass in the front seat." East was adamant that he wasn't about to be made to feel like anyone's chauffeur. He drew the line at the 'Do Boy' shit.

Sucking her teeth, Katori closed the door and East leaned over to open up the passenger side door for her. Getting in, she put her seatbelt on and turned her face to the window. "Can we stop at a Dunkin or Starbucks?" She asked with her head still in the same position.

"You gotta look at me when you talking, shorty. You always this rude?"

Turning, she stared at East. This time she took in all of his features that she didn't care to when she first encountered him. East had a warm, caramel skin tone that matched hers. His neck was tatted up and she noticed a small tattoo on the side of his forehead. Whoever he'd gone to for the art had done a beautiful job at not making the tattoos look rugged.

His eyes were deep, and expressive, with a hint of danger. It allowed Katori to see how he felt even if he didn't open his mouth. He was serious in his request, she gathered by his stare. His jawline was strong, with a perfect nose, and his lips were much like her own; big and suckable. Seeing that she'd gotten too caught up in her stare, she cleared her throat before speaking.

"Can we stop at a Dunkin or Starbucks?" She repeated. There was no need to get into it with him and cause Tae to have to defend her or go without breakfast on account of her attitude.

"Yeah. There's one before we hop on the highway."

"Preciate it," Tae said from the back seat.

"Don't mention it. Ay, where you go to school anyway?"

"I go to Lehman High School."

"Oh, aight. That's right there on East Tremont, right."

"Yeah."

"Cool. And where you gotta go? You don't look like you dressed for work."

"Don't worry bout me. I'll be getting out with him and going about my day as I normally would." He didn't need to know her plans.

"Man, you hell. How you gon' know how to get back to the crib?"

"I have it saved on my maps. You don't have to clock my moves, Eastland. We're not going back to the apartment and we won't be talking about what happened to anyone."

"I ain't trippin' over that. I just wanna make sure y 'all—. Nevermind, shorty. I'm gonna text you the address." He pulled into the drive-thru of the Starbucks and let them place their orders. East picked up on how polite and soft spoken Katori was with the Starbucks employee. He laughed inwardly at her. She caught his smile but played it off by not questioning it.

He drove up to the window where the chipper Starbucks employee gave them their $34 total. "Here, can you give this to her to scan?" Katori handed him her phone with the Starbucks app pulled up.

The woman scanned the phone and handed him their order, along with the receipt, and bid them a good day. East waited a few seconds for Katori to check the order and drove off once she thanked the lady for the food. Hopping on the highway, his phone rang. Seeing his mother's name on the caller ID, he connected the call via Bluetooth.

"Wassup, lady?"

"Hey, my handsome son. What you up to?"

"I'm in the streets. What you got going on?"

"Nothing much just finished making breakfast. You know what today is, right."

"Yep, Friday."

"Yes. October 13th, your sister's birthday. Are you going to call her and wish her a happy one?"

"I didn't plan on it, ma. But I'm assuming the reason for your call is because you want me to."

"Yes, I do. It would mean a lot to me."

East sighed. He could never tell his number one lady no and Ms. Evelyn knew that. Of course, he knew his sister's birthday was today. It had been the same day the last 26 years of his life. The only thing that changed was that they hadn't been close for the last two. Emersyn had some shit with her that East just chose not to be a part of. He loved her from a distance, but it had been established that should she ever want to get her shit together he'd be present and available when she called.

"**Aight, ma, I'll send her a text before the day is out.**" It was the most East was willing to do.

"**I'd prefer a call but if a text is all you have to offer at this time, I'll take what I can get.**"

"**It is and I appreciate you respecting my position. I'll give you a call once it's done. I already know how you do.**"

Ms. Evelyn chuckled. "**I'm glad you do. I love you, son.**"

"**I love you, too, lady.**" He ended the call and turned the music on.

He didn't know it, but Katori had been tuned into his conversation. By the brief interaction, she concluded that he had a good relationship with his mother. To Katori, a man's relationship with his mother said a lot about him as a person. It also spoke volumes for the way they treated women. She made sure to instill that in Tae even more now with their mother being gone.

"Y'all can let me out on the corner, and I'll walk the rest of the way," Tae said.

"You betta not be thinking bout skipping, Tae. I'm not playing."

"Man, ain't nobody skipping."

"Okay. Make sure you call me when you get out so I can tell you where to meet me. Bring Kita with you too, so we can have that talk."

"Aight, love you, Tori, and thanks for the ride, man."

"Ain't no thang, kidd," East replied as Tae stepped out of the car and walked down the block. "Now, where am I dropping you, gangsta?" He questioned, putting the car in drive.

"The next block over, thank you." Katori sipped her Grande Caramel Ribbon Crunch and looked straight ahead.

"I hope wherever you going you plan on putting that money up for safekeeping. It's crazy to be walking around with that much bread on you."

"Again, none of your concern, Eastland. I got me. Been having me for a while now. Right here." She pointed to the street. Pulling up to the curb, he stopped, and she hopped out quickly, leaving her banana nut bread behind. East didn't even bother calling her back to get it. Instead, he took a bite of the savory pastry and pulled off. *Good for her mean ass*, he thought to himself, finishing it in three bites.

KATORI KNOCKED on her best friend's door, bracing herself for the curse out that was sure to come. She was totally fine with it. She desperately needed to decompress and who better to do it with than her best bitch.

"Who is it?"

"Your best friend who loves you so very much."

"Oh, yeah, come on up in here so I can cuss you smooth out." Katori heard the locks turning before the door was snatched open. "I'm starting to think that this friendship don't mean as much as you say it do." Fatima stood at the door still dressed in her pj's, a silk bonnet on her head, and her morning mimosa in her hand.

"Don't do me. I got a lot going on."

Fatima moved to the side and nodded for Katori to enter. "Come on and let's deal with it. You want a morning pick me up?"

Walking inside, Katori took off her shoes and placed them on the shoe rack in the foyer. "No. I'm going to head to work when I leave here. You shouldn't be having one either. You gon' fuck around and burn one of your clients with them hot combs."

Fatima sipped her drink and rolled her eyes. "Girl, please. I need my morning mimosa to deal with them heffas that come up in here with all their stories. Shit drains me sometimes. Contrary to popular belief, stylists don't always wanna talk." Fatima was a hair stylist who specialized in natural hair and locs. She was the only person Katori trusted with her hair.

"Yea, but look, I don't have a lot of time. First, I need you to put this bag in your safe. It has my life savings in it, so I need you to hold onto it for me."

"Ohhkayy… but why do you need me to hold onto your savings when you have an apartment as well as a bank account, Tori?" Fatima was puzzled. There was no doubt that she was going to handle whatever her best friend needed her to handle, though.

Sighing, Katori plopped down on the couch and threw

her bags next to her. "Rob was killed yesterday over some street shit he was into. He was killed right in front of me and Tae. The person who did it gave us a choice to stay with the body and deal with the aftermath or come with him. I decided to go with him; a decision I'm still trying to wrap my head around. He offered us his condo to stay in until things blow over. He knew me and Tae by name, Tima. I'm sure he knows more about us than he's letting on, too. And that's not even the worst part of all this shit, the worst part is that I'm not scared to be around this man after what went down. Does that make me a fucked up person? If I wasn't me, I'd be judging the shit outta me right now."

As Katori rambled, Fatima stood in front of her, completely floored by the news she had just laid on her. She slowly sat down next to Katori and sat her drink down on the coffee table. "Girl, fuck all that other shit you talkin' bout, you witnessed a murder? And you talkin' bout going to work today? Where is Tae? This is some traumatic ass shit we talkin' bout, Katori."

Katori's head dropped. "I know. We dropped Tae off at school before I came here."

"Uhhh, we? You let the killer bring you here?" Fatima inquired, wanting to know if she should be prepared. She had a registered .9mm and knew how to use it should a situation arise.

"Hell, no. Just because I chose to be around him don't mean I'm involving anyone else."

"Okay, cool. But damn, Rob is dead. You don't seem

broken up about it. Explain that to me." In no way was Fatima judging her friend. She did, however, want to know where her head was with the situation.

Katori lifted her head and turned her body to Fatima. "I'm gonna be honest with you and it may sound off but it's real. This shit is still fresh, 24 hours ago fresh so, of course, it stings, and I'm hurt that he's dead. At the same time, there was some shit that was revealed to me this morning that put my mind in a whole other place, sis."

"The only thing I could think of is you finding out he cheated. That shit would fuck a bitch up." Fatima sipped her drink and picked up on Katori's silence. The fact that she had hit the nail on the head made Katori drop her head. "So, this is the part where you say, *bitch please.*" She gestured with her hands. Still, Katori stared but said nothing. "Damn, he did, didn't he?" Fatima caught on quickly and shook her head. She was too through.

"Yep, cheated, and apparently, he has a kid."

"Oooh, fuck no! His dead ass got some fucking nerve! A whole baby is out of control. How'd you find that out?"

Katori sucked her teeth. "His sister let it slip then tried to backtrack."

"That's fucked up. I hope you let that hoe have it." Katori couldn't tell who was more upset, her or Fatima.

"Nope. I let her make it. I gotta play my cards right with this one. Shit, according to her, me and Rob haven't been together. I'll keep it that way. I know no one will be looking for me or Tae to find out what we know about his death. I do

need to go back there and get the rest of our stuff, though."
Although Katori had told East that she wasn't going back to
the apartment, she wanted her stuff before Patrice or anyone
else could get to it.

"If I were you, I'd give it a few more days, Tori. Let shit
die down a little."

"Yeah, I guess you're right." Sighing, Katori stood to her
feet. "I'm gonna change for work. Please put this up for me."
She handed Fatima her knapsack.

"You know I got you, girl. Always." They shared a hug
that was much needed. Pulling back, Fatima wiped the lone
tear that fell down Katori's cheek. "You're not wrong, Tori.
You were put in a fucked up position and now you're moving
as you see fit. Things never just happen, there's always a
reason. You'll find out why you were led to make the choice
you made soon enough."

Katori didn't know what her best friend was getting at,
but she let her words sink in. She had no control over how
things would play out over the next few days or what life
would throw at her next for that matter. That said, she
planned to move accordingly and make sure she and Tae
stayed out the way.

Chapter 6

"Ooh, shit, eat that dick up, Tori," East moaned while guiding his eater's head up and down in the backseat of his car. It felt like she would make him buss this time. He knew that would be a great accomplishment for her seeing as no woman had ever made him nut from head alone. He felt his nut building up in his balls sack and then the feeling vanished. "The fuck?" He let out when she popped his dick out of her mouth.

"Who the hell is Tori?" Yanna looked up with fire in her eyes and a wet mouth.

"What?" East stared back at her, dumbfounded. Although it was Yanna's head in his lap, he couldn't get Katori's face out of his mind.

"Don't play dumb, East. You just called me another bitch name while your dick was halfway down my esophagus."

Yanna's pretty yellow face had turned a shade of red from being so mad.

"Damn. My bad, Yanna. It won't happen again." He gestured to his now semi-hard dick. "You ain't gon' handle that?"

She gave him an incredulous look and rolled her neck. "You gotta be out ya mind. I ain't bout to have lockjaw and you over here fantasizing bout the next bitch." She slid her thong back on along with her leggings and sat back in the seat, pouting.

"Aight." East tucked his dick back into the hole in his boxers and pulled his jeans up. He wasn't about to beg her for no head, and she knew that.

"Really?"

"Really, what? You know a nigga ain't trippin' over no head, Yanna. It's cool. I understand how you feel." He opened the door and got out. "Get in the front."

Walking around to the driver's seat, he got in and started the car up. He'd come by her place to fill out paperwork for his new business venture and they ended up in the backseat at her request. Yanna was East's fuck buddy and realtor. At least that's what he considered her. Her definition of the relationship may have been different, and East let her have it so long as she never came out of her body if she did see him with another female. And she knew she wasn't the only woman he fucked; she was, however the most consistent.

"So, Who's Tori?" Yanna questioned while taking her hair down from the bun she'd wrapped it in to get to the business.

"Someone I know." East didn't feel the need to expound on his response. He and Yanna didn't ask those kinds of questions to each other. Mainly because neither one of them owed the other an explanation as to how they moved. Again, something that East expected her to understand.

"Well, I know that. I don't think you'd call me by a name you didn't know. Hell, I didn't think you'd call me by another woman's name period, yet this Tori person came to mind."

"It was an accident. It'll never happen again. Is that the paperwork for me to sign?" He pointed to the folder that she had sat in the windshield when she first got in the car.

"Yes." Grabbing the folder, she opened it to go over its contents. She pointed to each place his signature would go on the document and he cross-checked everything they'd gone over previously. "You did it! After months of showing, you almost every commercial property in the Tri-State area, we're finally here."

East had found another business to funnel his money through that he knew would bring in twice as much as the coffee shop. He'd purchased a club for a sweet deal, thanks to Yanna's savviness and way with words.

"Yeah, but it was worth every tour, right." Reaching into his pocket, he pulled out a check and handed it to her.

Scanning the check, she smiled, nodded, and put it inside the folder. "It's always worth it when it comes to you, East. You know that." She gave him googly eyes that he ignored.

"Did you get in touch with your people to see when we can start construction?" East checked his watch and the time read 4:15 p.m. It was time for him to move on to his next stop.

"I did. They gave me a timeline of two months at the most. Being that this place was once a lounge you don't have to do much other than put your own spin on it. And with you being so meticulous and specific as to what you want, I'm confident that it'll get done in no time."

"Cool. Just make sure you're keeping me in the loop. If you need anything, don't hesitate to call."

"Anything?" She purred and flicked her tongue. Yanna was a high yellow chick, with a pretty face and a runner's body. A freak that often let East slut her out. She was open for him. East not wanting to pursue a relationship with her had nothing to do with Yanna and everything to do with the fact that he didn't feel drawn to her outside of sex. You couldn't force chemistry.

"Related to this business, yeah. As far as that pussy, you know I'll make it when I can."

"I just love when you pencil me in," she said sarcastically with a smile. Putting her hand on the door handle, she pushed it open. "Have a productive rest of the day. I'm gonna get these papers filed away for you."

"Thanks again, Yanna. I appreciate the work you put in, forreal."

She closed the door and leaned into his open window. "Yeah, appreciate me by not thinking bout the next chick when you're with me the next time." She blew him a kiss and walked off.

East shook his head and pulled off from the curb. He couldn't guarantee that Katori wouldn't invade his thoughts again. He couldn't understand why she'd become a permanent fixture in his head since seeing her picture in his office over a week ago. He couldn't say that he'd made an effort to shake the thoughts either. As he drove to his next destination, his phone rang. To his surprise, Katori's name appeared on the screen. He answered on the third ring.

"Wassup, mean ass?"

"Don't call me that. There's nothing mean about me." Her response was hostile and went along with his description of her.

"What you need Katori?"

"I don't need anything."

East snickered. **"Well, what you want then, woman?"**

"Can you pick up some stuff from the supermarket and drop it off at your place? I can cash app you."

"You must think a nigga an errand boy or something. You got me fucked up *Ms. I can take care of it.*" She sucked her teeth, and he could tell she was rolling those pretty eyes of hers. **"Man, send me the list, shorty."**

"Thank you." She still had a hint of attitude, but it was lighter. **"Can I hang up now?"**

"Yeah, smart ass."

"Send me your cash app."

"Aight." They hung up at the same time. East didn't have a cash app and even if he did, he wouldn't have sent it to her.

He'd pick up the groceries and cover the tab. It was just the type of nigga he was.

———

"AY, ma when you buy yo chicken wings, you buy them in the pack, or you buy the frozen joints right here?" East flipped his phone on the Facetime call to show his mother what he was referring to. He'd been in Trader Joe's for over an hour going through the list Katori had texted him.

He was convinced that this particular grocery store was a foreign place. While everything was organized, it was kind of overwhelming as it was so much shit to choose from. Further reminding East why he chose to Instacart or pick up his groceries after shopping from home. He could've called Katori to ask questions about the list she'd sent but with her mouth, he knew that it was highly likely that the end result would be him leaving the cart and leaving her lil ass hungry.

"Boy, what you doing in the Supermarket? And Trader Joe's at that. That place is for elite shoppers."

"And I ain't elite?"

She giggled. **"Elite meaning, they are familiar with grocery shopping and not from that app you use."**

"Oh, well, here I am tryna navigate this place. About these wings, though. Which one do you get?"

"I don't choose son. I usually get a pack each. Who you shopping for?"

He dropped both packs in the half-full cart and flipped

the camera back so that it was facing him. "**I have guests at my condo and I wanna make sure the fridge and pantry are stocked.**"

"**And they sent you to the store? Tuh, must be some special guests.**"

"**If you wanna put it that way.**" Referring back to the list for the last item and realizing what was written, he stopped the cart in the middle of the Health & Beauty aisle. "**Oh, hell no. She got me fucked up,**" he flipped, out loud.

"**Umm, excuse me, your mouth.**" His mother scolded and wagged her finger in the camera.

"**My bad, ma.**" Shaking his head, East pushed the cart through the aisle and up to the checkout line.

"**Did you find everything?**"

"**Yup. Everything I'm willing to get.**"

"**Have you reached out to your sister yet?**"

"**The day isn't over yet, ma. I didn't forget.**"

"Hi. Did you find everything okay?" The cashier greeted as he loaded the conveyor belt.

"I believe so."

The girl batted her eyes while slowly scanning the items.

"**I won't pressure you about it, then,**" his mother responded. "**And don't think I won't remember this the next time I ask you to go to the grocery store for me. I want the same kind of treatment that you're giving your mystery guests.**"

"**Ion know, ma. I can't promise you I'll be making**"

another supermarket run again. Y'all can have this. I'll buy your groceries, though, anytime."

"That'll be $225.27, handsome." She flashed all 32 of her teeth, displaying her gap.

"Oh, she ready to put it on the register, ain't she."

East laughed at his mother and watched the girl's face change from seductive to pure embarrassment. **"Let me handle this, ma. I love you."**

"Alright, I'll go. I love you, too." She hung up and East pulled out the cash he had in his pocket to pay. "Thank you, beautiful." He threw the cashier a compliment as a way to apologize for his mother calling her out.

"Have a good day," she replied.

East was happy to leave the store. He couldn't wait to get to Katori and tell her about herself. Loading the bags in his trunk, he decided to stop and pick up a pizza pie. He didn't know what Katori and Tae had planned for dinner but figured buying the pizza would be a nice gesture if Katori didn't feel like cooking. By the time he made it to the condo, it was a quarter to seven.

"One second, Mr. E," Paul said upon seeing East get out of his car and pop his trunk. Inside the building, he grabbed one of the carts used to help residents transport groceries should they need it.

"Good looking, Paul. How'd everything go today?"

"Everything went fine. She came back here with the brother and another female. They arrived in an Uber. Nothing looked suspicious."

East nodded. Katori never mentioned having anyone over and East knew he'd have to talk to her about unauthorized guests. He was fresh off a body and although Katori and Tae were technically strangers, he'd done his homework on the two. He didn't know the other person.

He held the pizza box in one hand and used the other to push the cart onto the elevator. Pressing his floor, he took out his phone to text his sister.

Me: Happy birthday, Emmy. I love you and hope you have a safe one.

Sliding his phone into his hoodie, he stepped off the elevator once he reached his floor. Knowing his sister, he wouldn't wait for a response back. Depending on what kind of mood she was in, Emersyn could text back thank you or ignore the message altogether. If she needed something though, East knew to expect a call from her. Punching in the code to enter the condo, he pushed the door open to find Tae and a young girl seated at the kitchen island while Katori stood before them in silence.

"Damn, who died?" He questioned, referring to the silence.

"Boy, nobody died," Katori responded, walking around the kitchen island and towards him. The young girl turned to where he could fully see her face and it appeared that she'd been crying. East didn't know what he'd walked into or if he even wanted to be privy to it. Whatever the situation was, it left the environment tense.

Chapter 7

"Can I talk to you for a second?" Katori asked East as she placed the bags on the kitchen counter.

"Yeah, let's talk."

"Tae, put the stuff for the fridge and freezer away," She instructed. "Anything that goes in the cabinet, leave it out."

"And I got that pie for y'all, so help yaselves."

"Good looking out." Tae got up along with Kita as Katori and East left the kitchen.

Katori led East to the bedroom she slept in and closed the door behind them.

"Who's the girl out there?" East asked her, standing with his back against the door.

"I brought you in here to tell you that, but I gotta know that it's safe to do so. You know, with everything that's already taken place."

East snickered at her response. "You don't think you sound crazy right now?"

"How so?" She cut her eyes at him. "We're fresh off an incident, are we not?"

"So, you don't know whether it's safe to tell me who you have in my crib, but you waited until you brought her all the way here to start feeling that way?"

Katori didn't respond right away. As she spoke, she knew her decision wasn't the smartest and although she didn't want to admit that she had moved reckless, she had to. "You're right. I could've handled it better and told you. This was a family emergency. Kita is my brother's girlfriend and I just wanna make sure she doesn't get caught up in no shit." She couldn't look him in his eyes. Katori hated to be wrong.

"That shit eating you alive, huh?" East playfully taunted her.

"What?" She looked up, rolling her eyes.

"Admitting that you were wrong."

"I'll admit that it does leave a bitter taste in my mouth, but hey," she shrugged, "If I'ma be the solid bitch I've been for the last 23 years, I gotta do what I gotta do."

"I like the way you think." East's eyes lingered on her a few seconds before he spoke again. "How'd you sleep last night?"

"I didn't. I have too much on my mind and those two in the living room have added to it."

"Oh, yeah? You wanna talk about it?"

"With you?" She gave him a questionable look.

East shook his head from side to side and looked over his shoulder. "Ion see nobody else in here girl."

"What you want with me, Eastland? You didn't have to put us up here. You could've easily taken us to a hotel, so what's really going on?"

East rubbed the back of his neck before pulling in, then releasing a slow breath. Katori speaking his full name made the hairs on his arms stand up. Hearing a woman say his name had never caused that reaction. "Why pay out of pocket when I have a place that I don't use?" He quickly recovered with a rebuttal. "Believe it or not, I'm really just tryna help. You may not like my method, but hey, I ain't holding y'all hostage. I ain't into that." His words and Katori's reality clearly didn't match up in her head.

"You just kill, huh?"

"Nah, I don't just kill, shorty. I stand on business."

"How'd you find out about me and my brother?"

"When someone becomes a problem, I make it my business to know everything about them. That includes those that are closely attached to them."

"Why'd you kill him in front of us? Was it your goal to traumatize me? Make us scared of you?"

"Are you?"

"Am I what?"

"Scared of me." It wasn't the image East was trying to portray so he hoped she said no.

"Oddly, no. Did what happened shake me up though, yes. I wouldn't be human if it didn't."

"You don't think I'm human?"

"I think you lack empathy." Her response was quick, as if she had anticipated his question.

"I'm empathetic, but not to bullshit."

"If you say so. How much were the groceries?"

"I took care of it. And speaking of taking care of it, you foul for what you put on there."

She smirked. "I take it that you didn't get the last thing I listed."

"Hell no. You outta pocket for even putting it on there."

Shaking her head, Katori walked towards him to leave out of the room. He moved aside, opening the door. "Crazy how you can kill somebody, but you can't pick up a box of Tampons." She left him standing in the doorway and headed back to the kitchen.

East watched as she walked off, piecing together the entire exchange in his head. He didn't know how long Katori and Tae's stay would last at his place, but he knew he wanted it to last long enough to get to know her more. There was something behind that tough exterior. Something that not even Rob was able to tap into during their relationship. East was confident that he'd figure it out soon enough. And whether it was under his roof or not, it would be her coming to him on her terms.

REENTERING THE KITCHEN, Katori found Kita and Tae hovered over the pizza box, stuffing their faces. When East walked in, Kita was in the middle of explaining how terrified she was of being responsible for another human being. Upon hearing the door opening, Katori hushed her. She didn't want East to know what all Tae had going on and she didn't want Kita to feel like she was putting her out there.

"Damn, I hope y'all left me a slice." Katori pulled the pizza box towards her, and her mouth watered at the huge slices.

"Yeah, we did. You know I can usually put away three at a time, but them slices big as hell," Tae commented. Standing up, he walked over to the counter to grab the roll of paper towels and handed them to Kita. "You aight?"

She nodded solemnly. "Yeah, I'm good. Katori, I—."

"Aight, if y'all straight, I'ma head out." East interrupted Kita's response as he headed towards the front door. "Come walk me out real quick, Katori. Hold it down Tae and nice to kinda meet you, shorty."

With a slice of pizza in her hand, Katori went to the door to let East out. "Thank you for getting the groceries. I know it may seem like we're getting comfortable but trust me, we're not." She wanted to let him know in not so many words that she didn't plan on being at his place for long.

"It's cool. Like I said, the door is open should you wanna leave. I just don't think it's a good idea at the moment. Oh, how you plan on getting Tae's girlfriend back home? You know, seeing as you don't have a car."

"But I do have Uber and Lyft. I got it handled."

"Aight. And another question, do you plan on attending Rob's funeral, if there's one?"

She shrugged her shoulders. "Not sure. Why you ask?"

"I think you should."

"You think I should?" She questioned, not understanding why he'd think it was a good idea.

"Yeah. It'll keep the heat off you and you'll have a reason to go back and collect the rest of your belongings." By her confused stare East could tell it either didn't make sense to her or she was trying to figure out his angle. "It's not something you have to do."

"I know. I can't wrap my head around it right now."

"Understandable. Should you decide that you're going to attend, let me know."

"Why?"

"So, I can make sure I'm in the vicinity."

She sucked her teeth. "I already told you that you don't have to worry about us speaking on what happened."

"And I told you I'm not worried about that."

"Okay, then why—."

"You love to go back and forth. I know you gave that nigga a run for his money with that mouth of yours."

"Whatever. Bye, Eastland."

"Have a goodnight, mean ass." He pulled the door closed and went on his way.

Putting his suggestion to the back of her mind, and storing it to come back to, Katori pressed forward to deal with what was in front of her. Right now, it was the baby situation between her brother and his girlfriend.

"Alright y'all, now that we don't have a stranger's ear around, let's figure this thing out. Talk to me, Kita."

Kita put her slice down in the box and used the paper towel Tae gave her to wipe her hands. Sighing, she glanced over at Tae before focusing back on Katori. "I can't have this baby. Y'all know my situation at home. I can't offer my child something that I don't have myself."

"And what's that?" Katori questioned.

"Stability." Her response tugged at Katori's heart, and she had to hold back her emotions. "I often don't know whether I'm coming or going to be honest. A baby doesn't need anyone who's merely just existing. If it wasn't for you and Tae, I would've checked out a long time ago."

Having heard all he could take, Tae got up from his seat and left the kitchen.

"Tae," Katori called out to him. "Tae."

"It's okay, Tori. I know why he left. He doesn't like to hear me speak my reality. And I hate to put it out there like that but it's the truth."

"And I get that, Kita. At the same time, don't make Tae what you have to live for. You are a beautiful, intelligent, and caring young woman. Your future is bright. You gotta see pass your current situation. And if anyone knows that it's often easier said than done, it's me. Trust me, I'm doing it as we speak."

Tears fell from Kita's face, and she didn't bother wiping

them. She felt like the world was on her shoulders, but she appreciated Katori's encouraging words.

"Are you sure about your decision?"

Sniffling, Kita wiped her face with her shirt. "I'm sure. I don't wanna ruin your brother's life. I really love Dontae."

"Everything's gonna be okay." Katori walked around and pulled her in for a hug. "I got y'all." Kita nodded. Since she'd known Katori, she had always kept her word, and came through.

Tae eventually came back to the kitchen after a few minutes and apologized for his abrupt exit. Kita explained her plan to terminate the pregnancy and he felt a twinge of sadness but knew it was the best decision for the both of them. Katori agreed to make the appointment and be present with Kita the day of and if she needed her after. The trio lounged around the condo for another hour before leaving to drop Kita home. Katori made sure to take her right to her front door while Tae chose to wait in the Uber.

He knew Kita's aunt didn't like him and didn't want to give her any reason to get down on her. He'd shared a few stories with Katori and Kita had mentioned how foul her aunt and cousins were. Had it not been for Tae assuring Katori that she didn't have to intervene on his behalf, she would've been on Kita's aunt's head a while ago. Kita didn't get a chance to put her hand up and knock before the door was snatched open.

"And just who the fuck do you think you are coming in here at this time of night?" Kita's overweight, greasy faced aunt stood at the door in a tattered robe that she could barely hold close due to her size, and a bandana tied tightly on her head the way 2Pac used to wear his.

"I was out with Tae and his sister," Kita spoke. Katori could tell she was embarrassed.

"You know don't nobody come up in this motherfucka late but the people who pay bills. I don't give a damn if Jesus himself escorted you home. Get your ass in here!"

Kita remained still and Katori rubbing her back was the only thing that pushed her forward after a few seconds. Once she was in the house, Tori spoke. "Look, I'm not privy to your family dynamics but the way you just handled that was unnecessary. Kita is a good kid and she's loving. Having a family that actually gives a fuck would definitely make life a bit easier for her." Katori knew she may have been overstepping, but she couldn't stand around saying nothing after what she'd witnessed.

Kita's aunt's head jerked, and she stepped out of her doorway. "What goes on in my house with any child under my care is my goddamn business. Kita can fool you with that good girl act but she's a product of my sister who was fast just like her. So, if I wanna cuss her ass out about coming in my shit late, I'll do just that."

"You right, this is your house, but out here is a street that the city of New York pays for. Understand that if you keep fucking with her, I'ma drag you up and down this bitch. You have a goodnight."

Katori was smaller in stature when it came to Kita's aunt,

but she meant everything she said. After a few seconds of a stare down between the two, Katori turned and made her way back to Tae and the Uber that awaited her. Inside the Uber, Tae was quiet.

"I'm glad you don't come over here to chill with her anymore. I should've dragged her aunt's big ass a long time ago."

"Thanks, Tori."

She looked over at her brother. "What you thanking me for?"

"Always coming through for me. You know, with mommy being gone, you're the only parent I have. I know it's not always easy on you, especially as I get older, and we run into these kinds of mishaps. I just want you to know that I appreciate you stepping in to make sure I'm straight. I don't know what I 'ma do when you start a family of your own."

"Boy, please." She mushed his head while giggling and wiping her wet eyes. "I'm not having no kids. Trust me, having you is enough." The thought of being a mom never crossed Katori's mind. She had so much she wanted to accomplish before then.

"You will," Tae assured her. "The right man will come along, and with my approval of course," he smiled, "y 'all gon make it happen."

"Boy, go head." Waving him off, Katori leaned her head up against the window. Between work, putting out Tae's fire, and thoughts of Rob's secret kid occupying her day, her body and mind needed rest.

Chapter 8

"I wanna leave it out for the next few weeks," Katori said to Fatima after her braids were taken out and her shoulder length locs styled. She loved her locs and how she was able to be versatile with them.

Today was Rob's funeral and at the last minute, she decided that she would attend. Not that she had been invited. Katori had been scrolling on her Facebook page and seen a post from a mutual friend detailing the funeral arrangements. She wasn't surprised that Patrice hadn't told her about it. And if she was being honest with herself, she could admit that she felt slighted. But, Katori was going to show her face, pay what little respect she had left for Rob and keep it moving.

It had been a week since she and Tae had been staying at East's condo. And while Tae was becoming comfortable,

Katori was still in plan mode. She figured once the funeral had passed, she'd be able to fully move forward. They hadn't seen much of East over the last week, and she found herself wondering why. It was odd to her at first when he popped into her head as she watched a Tubi movie about a woman who was kidnapped and fell for her kidnapper. Katori judged the woman throughout the whole movie and at the same time found herself blushing at the way the man and woman interacted with each other even when they were at each other's throats.

"What you smiling about?" Fatima asked, pulling the cape off of her and placing it on her rolling rack.

"Nothing. What you think about my outfit?" Katori stood up from the chair and ran her hands down the knitted black dress she wore. The dress was fitted, outlining her every curve.

"Your whole look is befitting for the occasion. It says, *I'm coming to pay my respects and at the same time show you bitches while I still ain't nothing to play with.*"

"That's not the look I'm going for, though." Katori smirked and walked over to the front door to grab her heels and jacket.

"Well, that's what it's saying, boo. And that is quite alright. Now, are you sure you wanna do this?"

"I do. It's gonna be closure for me. I also think it's only right for me to be there, if that makes sense. You don't have to come with me if you don't want to, Tima."

"Girl, please, I'm coming. And I understand why you

want to. Let me go grab my sneakers, though. I wanna be prepared in the event a bitch even looks at you funny."

"Yoooo, get outta my head. I'm over here planning in case shit go left."

"Shit, you already know."

"Where y'all going?" Tae questioned, walking from the back of Fatima's apartment, wiping sleep from his eyes.

"Rob's funeral." Katori hadn't told him about the funeral because she didn't want him to come with her. She didn't want Tae involved in no shit and she knew for sure that her brother was gonna step behind her no matter the situation.

"Why you ain't tell me?"

"Cause I don't want you to be there. I won't be there long."

Tae sucked his teeth. "Tori, I ain't no little kid. I done seen this nigga get a bullet put in his head, I'm sure attending the funeral won't traumatize me."

"And you won't miss anything either. I won't be gone long. Come on, Tima."

Mumbling something under his breath, Tae turned and walked away.

"Morning," Fatima greeted as she passed him in the hallway on her way back to the living room. He gave her a dry response and entered her guest bedroom, closing the door behind him. "Oop, what you do to my boy?"

"Nothing. He's mad because I didn't tell him about the funeral."

"Ohh, you know he's protective of you."

"I know. Come on, let's get this over with."

THE FUNERAL WAS HELD at Rob's family home church, Paradise Baptist Church in Manhattan. They had arrived just as the funeral services started and it was packed. Rob came from a big family, but Katori had only met a few people in the years they'd been together. She reasoned that it was because he wasn't close to his family and never brought it up. Seeing the way people had showed up for him, she thought to herself that there was no way that Rob had this many people and had no connection to majority of them.

Just as Katori decided that she and Fatima would stand close to the exit for the service, one of the parishioners walked over and asked if they wanted to sit. Fatima looked to Tori for her response and her eyes scanned the room to see where they could sit that gave them a clear path for the exit. Seeing none, she smiled and told the parishioner that they were fine standing. Nodding, the woman walked off, and the preacher called Patrice up to speak. She was dressed in a black pantsuit with a big, black hat on her head.

"The hat is taking me out," Fatima whispered and Katori elbowed her softly.

"Shut up."

Stepping up to the podium, Patrice cleared her throat. "Umm... I never thought that I'd be here before all of you today burying my little brother. Some people call this a funeral, other's call it a homegoing, as for me, I call it the worst day of my life." Patrice sniffled and someone called out from the crowd for her to take her time. "Rob was a lot of things funny, charismatic, loving, and most of all, he was loyal. He loved on the people close to him and he held them down. He didn't do people dirty. He stood ten toes down and the people that knew him know that for a fact. I hate that someone took him from me, from his family, but I'm even more angry that he was taken away from his son before he had a chance to watch him grow. My brother always wanted children and when he called me a year ago to tell me that he and Karmen were expecting a baby, he was so proud. The day she gave birth, and he called me on FaceTime to show me my handsome nephew, he was proud. So, while he was taken from us, he also left his little one here for our village to raise and we plan to do just that."

With each word that Patrice spoke, Katori felt her anger rising. She seethed as Patrice stood before the crowd and spewed lies about her brother being loyal after detailing what seemed like a planned pregnancy while he was in a relationship with her. Katori didn't know her hands were shaking until Fatima grabbed a hold of the left one. It was like her body had gone numb and all she heard was the echo of Fatima's voice. She continued to look on as Patrice stepped down and went over to her seat, in the front of the church.

While the church was packed, Katori had a full view of the front and watched as a woman stood and handed Patrice a small kid. She didn't need anyone to confirm that it was the Karmen person mentioned and the kid was Rob's son.

"Tori, let's go," Fatima whispered directly into her ear. "This is too much."

Katori's feet didn't move, nor did she acknowledge Fatima's request immediately. She wanted to stay and watch the whole shit show as it played out. Even though she knew that it would only build onto the anger that was mounting.

"I'm not leaving," she simply stated. Fatima felt her energy and looked straight ahead while keeping her hand locked with Katori's as a signal to let her know, she had her.

The rest of the funeral was a blur and once it was over, Katori was deep in her feelings and Rob's betrayal ate at her something serious. It wasn't just the fact that he'd cheated because in her mind, no man was faithful. It was the way in which he chose to carry on in their relationship, bashing her for not wanting to have a child just to step out and have a baby on her. At that moment, a lightbulb went off in her head. Katori only knew one side of the man she'd given four years of her life to. Years that she couldn't recoup.

As the pallbearers carried Rob out, Patrice and the rest of the family followed. She hugged people while walking through the aisle and stopped short when she noticed Katori. The look on Patrice's face said it all and time stood still as people walked around her and outside. Katori was sure that the scowl on her face said everything that she felt. Her gaze then went to the little boy who lay on Patrice's shoulder.

Carefully examining his facial features, Katori knew she

would be a fool to challenge the paternity of the child. He had Rob's whole face, down to the bushy eyebrows that always seemed unkept.

"Really, Patrice, you said you didn't invite her." The Karmen person made her way over and by her disposition, she wasn't happy about Katori's presence.

"I didn't invite her, Karmen," Patrice spoke, shifting her nephew to her other hip.

One thing Katori hated was for someone to know her by face and she have absolutely no idea who they were. It made her feel uneasy. And judging by Patrice's response, Katori knew that she was the person who'd made her existence known to Karmen.

"So, why is she here?"

"I came to pay my respects just like everyone else." Katori's tone was calm and didn't reflect her internal rage. "I believe I've reserved that right after being with someone for four years. Correct me if I'm wrong, Patrice." It wasn't in Katori's nature to be messy, but she wasn't about to dumb down who she was or the role she played in Rob's life when he was alive for anyone.

"Oh, you're counting the last two years?" The baby mother challenged. "Because that would be crazy, considering that we were together pretty much every day."

"But were you together every night? Or did you sleep in a cold bed with a wet pussy after he crept out of it?" Katori took a step forward and Fatima did the same. She hadn't spoken a word, she just stood near her friend, ready for whatever. "See, I didn't come here on that type of time and its clear to me that you know of me through whatever information you've been given, but you don't know me. However, Patrice does, and she knows that there's two places I ain't going with no female and that's back and forth. Congrats on your son. I hope that village she spoke of," she pointed to Patrice, "helps to raise him to be nothing like his dad."

With nothing left to say, Katori and Fatima casually made their exit. Katori had no expectations when she decided to attend the funeral. She didn't expect to be welcomed with open arms, she didn't expect to be acknowledged and escorted up to the front row with the rest of the family, and she didn't want any special treatment. She'd come for her conscious and to face the reality that what she thought she'd shared with Rob, he openly gave to someone else. Stepping outside at the very moment that Rob's casket was put in the back of the hearse, East's words rang loudly, *just be glad you ain't procreate with him.*

She went to say something to Fatima when they were approached by a group of four women, led by Rob's baby mother. Already on guard from the interaction in the church, Katori took off her earrings and Fatima followed suit.

"What we doing?" Katori spoke once the group was close.

"Shit, you tell me," Rob's baby mother pushed. "You showed up here unannounced, trying to throw around a timeline like that somehow defends your title. I know it must hurt seeing his new bitch and the son he always wanted sitting front row with the family. The family he never cared to introduce you to."

Katori turned to Fatima, confused. "Is she stupid or dumb?"

Fatima shrugged. "Ion know, sis. Its looking like both to me."

"Gotta be." Katori focused back on the people in front of her. "Girl, I'm not about to sit up here and argue with you about a front row seat at the funeral of a nigga who ate my ass daily. You got the baby, girl. You're clearly the winner. Or the biggest loser, depending on if you're looking at your glass half empty or half full."

"I didn't only get the baby. I got the ring, too." She flashed her ring finger, on her left hand. Still, Katori remained unfazed and unimpressed by the small stone on her finger. "And now, you and your brother will go back to being hom —."

She didn't get to finish her sentence before Katori's fist went crashing into her mouth. "Bitch, you got me so fucked up!" Katori yelled out, pulling Karmen to the ground." All of the pent-up aggression she had in her came spilling out as she pummeled Karmen's face.

Karmen represented the fire that had left her motherless, she represented Rob's deceit, and a multitude of other things that Katori had built up inside of her that she had yet to properly deal with. She could hear the ruckus around her but didn't tap back into her surroundings until she felt her hair being pulled.

"Bitch, get off my sister," a woman growled from behind Katori.

The grip that the woman had on Katori's head was tight, but it did nothing to stop the blows to Karmen's face. What did make her let up were the gunshots that rang out, followed by the screams of the woman who had her hair.

"Back the fuck up, shorty!" Katori heard East's menacing voice, then felt herself being swooped up in the air.

"This shit ain't over! Bum ass bitches wanna jump somebody, I'ma show y'all!" Fatima threatened as she was carried away in the same manner as Katori, only she was fighting to get out of the man's embrace that Katori didn't recognize. "Get off me, Trill!"

Katori said nothing as East held onto her and walked her over to his car, gun that he'd let off still in hand. The crowd of family members were all in disarray while the hearse with Rob's body had sped off. Police sirens could be heard in the distance as East put her in the passenger seat while the guy that had Fatima got in the back along with her.

"Y'all got me fucked up. I'm going back out there!" Fatima reached for the door handle and East pulled off. She hit the door hard and East slammed the brakes in the middle of the street, making everyone jerk forward.

"Tima, don't piss me the fuck off alright! Don't hit my shit again."

"Shut up, Eastland!" She shouted back and he pulled off again. Katori didn't even think to question how they knew each other. Her head was in a fog. "You good, Tori?"

"She hardheaded as fuck, I know that." Katori whipped her head in East's direction, and he matched her hard stare. "What? I told your hardheaded ass to let me know if you were going to the funeral for this exact reason."

"I don't have to run shit by you, Eastland! I'm grown and you ain't my daddy or my man! Yo ass ain't even been around in the last week so when was I gonna tell you."

"Yo fingers ain't broke. You could've called or sent me a text."

"Shut up talking to me right now. It's really not the time."

"Hold on," Fatima said from the backseat, "how y'all even know each other? Wait, this the… girl, why you ain't tell me my cousin was dude?"

Katori looked at Fatima through the rearview mirror. "Obviously because I didn't know he was your cousin, crazy."

"This is crazy! East," Fatima hit him in the back of the head, "why you ain't tell me you knew my best friend."

"Stop putting your hands on me for I put yo ass out my car, Tima. And I ain't tell you cause I ain't know y'all were friends. You don't come around our people like that." Fatima became quiet and sat back.

"You can drop us off to my house." Fatima was less animated than she had been.

The car was quiet for the rest of the drive, and it was needed. Katori was still very much in her feelings and not about the fight. She was trying to control the sudden butterflies in her stomach from being around East. She watched as he drove with a tight grip on the steering wheel and his jaw twitched. *You can be mad all you want,* she thought to herself while rolling her eyes. As they neared Fatima's place, the sounds of a police car could be heard close behind them.

"Give me your gun," Katori said to East as he pulled the car over on a side street.

"No," he responded.

"Eastland!" She called out his name sharply, making him look directly at her. "Give me your gun." He pulled it from his hip and handed it over to her. She quickly wrapped the headscarf she carried in her purse around the gun and laid it flat inside her bag. Katori didn't know what the outcome of the stop would be, she just silently prayed that she made it back home to her brother.

Chapter 9

*E*ast turned off the ignition to his car and glanced in the side mirror to see the officer step out of the police cruiser. He wasn't the least bit nervous, but he knew how Trill felt about cops and with Katori having tucked his gun away, he wanted to make sure that he maintained his composure and didn't give the officers any reason to search the car. Rolling down the window just as the officer approached the car, East took a deep breath. No matter how much money he had, it never changed the fact that he was just a nigga with money, emphasis on the nigga.

"Afternoon, can I see your license and registration, please."

"May I ask why you pulled us over?" East questioned before making an attempt to reach for his documents.

"Well, that is your right, isn't it?" By the officer's response, East could sense he was about to be on bullshit. "This vehicle matches the description of one that fled the scene of a funeral that was shot up not too long ago. Apparently, there was some kind of brawl amongst a few females as well. You mind letting your window down a little more so I can get a look at everyone."

East wanted to protest but knew if he did, it would only make the cop suspicious. He rolled his window down along with the back passenger. Reaching over Katori, he pulled his registration and spare license out of the glove compartment. Handing it over to the officer, he waited for further instructions.

"Give me a second to check everything out."

"We good, Jonathan," Fatima said, calling Trill by his government name once the cop was away from the car.

"Yeah, bro, this shit gon' be quick, don't even trip." Trill didn't respond to East or Fatima. He kept his hands balled up in a fist, on his lap.

"This bitch," Katori cussed lowly and tapped East.

"What happened?"

"Look." She held the phone up for him to see.

Patrice: The fact that you would come to my brother's funeral and pull this stunt is low, Katori. I don't think highly of you, but I would've thought you were better than that. Just know that the authorities have been alerted and you'll pay for today, I promise you.

"I'll take care of it," East said as the officer returned back to his car, only this time, he was accompanied by a female officer who walked over to Katori's side.

"I need all of you to step out of the vehicle."

"Step out? The hell going on, man?" Frustration was written on East's face and his voice was laced with anger.

"Your tags match the vehicle that was reported to our dispatcher. Please, everyone, exit the vehicle. Let's not make this difficult."

"Wait, what?" Fatima questioned, nervously. She had adjusted her octave to a lower level so as to not escalate the situation.

Wanting to avoid being forcibly removed from the car, Katori quietly and carefully stepped out of the car with her bag still in hand.

"This some bullshit," Trill whispered harshly, pushing his door open and slamming it closed. East couldn't even be mad at him.

"Just a quick search and you'll be on your way. Please step over to the sidewalk, next to the officer." Although the guy wasn't giving them a hard time, East was still pissed, and it showed all in his face.

While the male officer searched his car, he kept stealing glances at Katori. She hadn't moved her head once to look in his direction. In fact, she was so still, he wondered if she'd stopped her breath in the moment. Without thinking, he reached out and rubbed her arm. The gesture made her glance over at him. He nodded and she responded with a nod of her own. East whispered for her to stay calm, but that was better said than done, considering she was the one holding the gun in her bag.

"All clear. No weapons in the vehicle," the officer who searched the car stated. "You all are free to go."

Declining to respond, the foursome hopped back in the car. Katori didn't breathe a sigh of relief until the officers got back in their police cruiser and slowly drove off.

"Man, get me the fuck from round here," Trill let out from the backseat. He didn't have to tell East twice.

East peeled off, making it to the front of Fatima's building in minutes. Trill was the first to hop out of the car, followed by Fatima. East knew his boy needed a minute and with the bond Trill and Fatima had growing up, East knew she would be able to get his mind right.

"Here you go," Katori spoke, grabbing his attention and handing him his gun with her scarf still wrapped around it.

"Why'd you do that?" He tucked the gun away and placed the scarf in her lap.

"Felt like it was the right thing to do in the moment. And I owe you for stepping in back there. Even though you kind of did the most with all that yelling."

"Man, you got me so tight, seeing you out there squabbling with them bitches. In a dress at that. Then my cousin out there witchu. Y'all bugged out." East shook his head.

"You don't even know why we were fighting, Eastland."

"It doesn't matter. You ain't no ghetto rat, so you don't do what they do. Same goes for Tima with her crazy ass. How long you been friends with my cousin anyway?"

"A few years. And I've been around her immediate family. I've never seen you."

"I'm not a person that likes to be seen. I just make sure my presence is felt when I do come around." Katori stared at him for a few seconds. She still found herself trying to figure him out. "What?"

"You're one odd man, you know that."

"And you are one mean woman."

"I'm not mean. I'm misunderstood."

"Maybe. And if you are, it's because of how you show up."

"Excuse me? You haven't been around me long enough to know how I show up."

East smirked. "Shorty, when I first met you, you had on a shirt that said FUCK OFF."

"First of all, we never really met. At least that's not how I see it. And just because I don't easily fall into conversation with people, it doesn't make me mean. I'm just not much of a people person. Life and its circumstances have made me this way."

"You think you just said something, huh?"

"What?" Katori scrunched her face up.

"You said all that to use as an excuse for coming off as a… and excuse my language…a bitch."

Katori's mouth dropped open. In all of her 23 years of living, no man had ever called her out her name and she didn't let them have it. "And that's where we meet the end of this conversation and I get out your car before I cuss you the fuck out!" She reached for the door handle and went to push the door open.

East grabbed her other hand. "Hol' on, hol' on."

"Nigga, let me go!" She snatched her hand back from him and got out the car.

"Let me take you out to dinner!" He shouted out the window.

"Boy, go ta hell!" She shouted back, giving him the finger.

East just smiled. It was the second time he'd gotten her to have some kind of conversation with her. Katori didn't know it, but East liked that she was standoffish and mean. It only meant that he didn't have to deal with other dudes in her face. He wanted Katori for himself.

"I CAN'T BELIEVE that this guy that you've been shacking up with for the last week is my cousin. That is wild," Fatima said, entering her apartment and holding the door open for Katori to walk through.

"I'm not shacking up with nobody. That would imply that we are somehow together, which we're not. Me and Tae are about to be up outta there by next week, too."

"Why?"

"Well, that's a dumb question, Fatima."

"Hol' on now, heffa. I know you may still be in your feelings about what happened but all that," she gestured with her hands, "is being directed in the wrong direction."

"Whatever. I'm about to change my clothes so we can go." Katori was deep in her feelings and East calling her out didn't make it any better.

"Not you being deadass wrong and tryna be strong about it." Much like her cousin, Fatima wasn't easily deterred by her best friend's attitude. And being that she'd been around longer, she knew when Katori was bothered by something.

Katori stopped in the middle of the living room and turned to Fatima. "Tima, I was really at a funeral fighting my nigga secret baby mother."

"I know, I was there."

"That shit is insane. This nigga waits to die to start causing problems. Where they do that at?"

"Shit, hell if I know. Them bitches still gotta see me, though. And I'm talking on sight type shit." Fatima felt herself getting mad all over again.

"And then your cousin just further pissed me off. Do you know he called me a bitch." Fatima put her hand up to her mouth and snickered "That shit is not funny."

"Well, friend, you are a little bitchy at times. I mean, look at how you just snapped at me."

"I didn't mean to come off that way, so for that, I apologize."

"I know. You just be in your head and sometimes I gotta bring you back. Come on, let's get some wine." Taking off their coats and dropping them on the couch, they walked into the kitchen.

"You think I'm mean?" Katori sat up on the barstool and folded her hands across her chest.

"Mean, no. Stubborn and standoffish, yes. And I say that with love."

"You can be a little rude sometimes, too, sis and a little too honest." Tae came around the corner and entered the kitchen.

"There's no such thing as too honest," Katori countered. "And really, Tae?" She was shocked to find out her brother felt the same. "So, y'all both think I'm a bitch?"

"Yo' eavesdropping ass," Fatima said to a smiling Tae. "Girl, that is not what either of us said but somehow that's what you heard."

"Why y 'all look like y'all been fighting?" Tae inquired, taking a seat next to his sister.

"Because we have," Katori answered. "That's a small thing to a giant, though. Stick to the topic at hand, y'all thinking I'm a bitch."

"Again, we didn't say thattttt," Fatima sang, while pouring a glass of wine and placing it in front of Katori. "Drink, you need it."

"Well, I grew up with you being this way and love you just the way you are. People don't know the other side of you. The nurturing side of you. They only know the person you show them, sis."

"Which is the person who is often standoffish," Fatima added.

"I'm just guarded and today further proves the reason

why I have to be. I gotta be selective of who I give my energy to and who I allow in my space. You see how the nigga I laid next to the last few years did me."

"I'm lost," Tae said. "What happened?"

"Rob cheated and has a son."

"Word? I'm sorry, sis. You good?"

"Yep," Katori replied without giving it any thought.

Tae wanted to ask more questions but knew not to pry. His phone rang and he excused himself from the conversation.

"Are you sure?" Fatima questioned, sipping her wine.

"About?"

"You being good."

"Yeah. Of course, I gotta fully process everything as the days come but, I'll be straight."

"You know I'll be here every step of the way and maybe… just maybe you'll let my cousin be there, too." Fatima slid out of the kitchen quickly after her statement.

Katori picked up her wine glass and downed the sweet drink in one swallow. She didn't need East to help her process. The only thing he was going to do was help himself into getting cussed out when she saw him again.

Chapter 10

East had a feeling that Katori would be at Rob's funeral, and he was glad that he went with his gut to have Trill get the location for the service ahead of time. He'd arrived along with Trill just a few minutes before Katori and Fatima showed up. He was surprised to see his cousin by her side. He hadn't seen Fatima in a while. She was related to his father's side of the family and mainly stayed to herself by choice. Unlike with his sister, Fatima wasn't into any bullshit, she just chose to do her own thing. Either way, it was always love between the two of them.

When he saw the duo walk up the block, he watched the way Katori moved. She wasn't trying to draw attention to herself, and she moved like she was just a friend coming to pay her respects. Not that he expected her to be falling all over the place, but he liked that she moved with poise. Even with her calm and cool demeanor, East was already prepared in case things went left and they did. Only, he didn't expect for Katori to throw the first punch.

The way she beat on Rob's baby mother, he knew the woman couldn't take much more. And Katori wasn't pulling hair, she was throwing punches like a man. East let her get off for a few until he saw another female jump in, followed by two on one where Fatima was holding her own. At that point, he decided to clear the whole scene with a few shots in the air. Everyone scattered like he knew they would, and he yanked the chick off Katori, snatched her up, and forced her to the car. The way he reacted; it would've been easy to mistake Katori for his woman.

Later that night, after chilling with Trill, East headed home to change clothes and switch cars. His Audi was hot after being pulled over by the police and he didn't want to continue driving the car with the same tags that had been ran through the system. The inconvenience of it all made him even more mad. It was clear that snitching was a common thing amongst Rob's people. And unfortunately, one thing East hated more than a snitch was a thief; Rob just so happened to be both.

"Hey, Siri, call Martinique," East commanded his phone. The phone rang a few times before connecting.

"When and where?" The female on the other line answered, sounding half asleep.

"Baychester Plaza. You think you can make it there in an hour?"

"Dammit, East. I hate when you do this shit on such short notice. How many of us do you need?"

"Just two, Nique. And you know I'll compensate you for your time."

"Alright. Text me the full address and description of the person."

"My girl. Love you."

"Yeah, yeah." The call disconnected and he called Fatima next.

"Hey, cousin," she greeted.

"Wassup, you good over there?"

"Boy, cut the bullshit. You only calling to see if Katori's good and she is. She's actually sleeping right here on the couch. Hold on, lemme go in my room." Fatima got up off the couch and tip toed to her room. "Okay, go head."

"I was calling to check on both of y'all. I would've called her mean ass but I know she still mad about earlier."

"Cause she thinks you called her a bitch."

"And I didn't. I said it's the way she presents herself. That's your girl, I'm sure you know that." If East was anything, he was honest.

"And as with any woman, you know we hate to be told about ourselves."

"Yeah, well, you know me. Woman, man, child, cripple, or crazy, I'ma call it like I see it."

"You like my friend, huh?"

"You can tell?"

"I would assume that you ain't letting nobody stay at your place that you don't like. You're quite the generous kidnapper aren't you." Fatima giggled.

"Man, tell your friend ain't nobody kidnap her ass. She's free to come and go as she please."

"Mmhmm. Anyway, is Trill okay?"

"Yeah. My boy straight. I see you still got that soft spot for him." Fatima made East promise a long time ago that he'd never bring up her past with Trill.

"Don't go there, Eastland. I just wanted to make sure he was alright."

"Aight. But ay, I need you to do me a solid."

"I'm not playing matchmaker. If you're interested, then you need to put the work in."

"I am. I wanna make her dinner."

"Oh, hell naw. I draw the line at you trying to poison my girl."

East cracked up at the switch in Fatima's tone. "Ain't nobody tryna poison her. I'ma have my mama walk me through something quick."

"Ok," Fatima responded, skeptical. "What you need me to do?"

"Keep her over there for the next two hours. I'm gonna go whip everything up then swing back your way to pick her and Tae up."

"Tae not here."

"Oh, aight. Can you do that for me though."

"Ummm, I guess I can. And I'm warning you now, she's

going to give you a hard time, but don't let it deter you. She has a wall up for good reason, but she is a dope ass person. She's loyal, trustworthy, and you can count on her. She gon stand ten toes down on her shit."

East thought back to earlier when Katori asked for his gun. Her reasoning was because she felt like it was the right thing to do. She didn't have to put herself on the line, but she stuck her neck out for him anyway. That was some real shit.

"Good looking out, cuz. And before I let you go, that shit that happened back at the funeral will be taken care of. I put Martinique on it."

"Oh, you put crazy on it, sheesh. I planned to see them bitches, but Nique bout to do them filthy."

Martinique was East's god sister and a certified bully. Whenever he had a situation involving a female and needed someone who didn't think about consequences, he called her. Nique slept, ate, and breathed violence. She never needed to know the why, just the where and when. It worked out in East's favor every time.

"That she is. But, let me go so I have enough time to do what I gotta do. Thanks again, Tima. I hope this means I'll be seeing more you, cuz."

"Me, too. Love you."

"Love you, too."

East ended the call and headed for his mother's house. If anyone was going to help him prepare a meal, it would be her. Plus, he knew he needed to be monitored. He was sure that if he attempted to make anything at his crib, he'd be getting a visit from the fire department.

WHEN EAST ARRIVED at his mother's house, he was surprised to see his sister in the living room, asleep on the couch. He'd used his key to let himself in and it was the one time he wished that he'd called his mother before he came over. Emersyn was snuggled up on the plush, oversized couch he had purchased with a hood over her head, hiding her face. With her being a heavy sleeper, she didn't hear East come through the door or walk over to her. Upon further inspection, he was able to see why she had the hood on in the house. Emersyn's right eye was black and blue, and the left eye looked like it was in the process of healing.

Shaking his head, he walked out of the living room as quiet as he came and went to find his mother. He could hear smooth jazz coming from the kitchen, so he headed there. In the kitchen, Ms. Evelyn hummed a tune, while standing at the sink.

"Hey, ma," he greeted. His energy was now off after seeing his sister.

Ms. Evelyn turned around, wiping her hands on her apron. "Hey, son." She had a somber tone, and her body language mirrored it. Normally, she would be at the door to greet her son as soon as her security system alerted her, but tonight, Ms. Evelyn's heart was heavy. And she knew that

East wasn't going to make things any better with his straight forwardness. "What brings you by?"

"I needed your help with something, but it looks like you have your hands full so don't even worry bout it." He kissed her on the cheek and leaned against her pantry door. "How was your day?"

She looked passed him, out into the living room before answering. "It wasn't the best, but I still made sure to thank God for another day above ground."

"Yeah, gotta make sure we do that on the daily. People out here moving so reckless, it's hard to believe that they even value life, forreal." East grabbed an apple from the fruit basket on the counter and took a bite.

"Some people aren't moving reckless, Eastland. Some people are in situations and doing the best they can with the cards they've been dealt."

"Most times that's a choice, ma. People make choices." They both knew they were referring to Emersyn's situation without really speaking on it. "That's just my opinion, though."

"So, what do you suggest we do, Eastland?"

"About what?"

"Boy, don't piss me off. What do we do about your sister?"

"Nothing." East took another bite of the apple and shrugged his shoulders. "I had to wash my hands of the situation, ma. How many times I'ma beat a nigga up, send him to the hospital, only for her to nurse him back to health, just for him to lump her shit up? I told y'all, the next time I get a call about that nigga, I'm putting him in the ground and that's on big God. Shit, the way Emmy act, she may fuck around and get me locked up if it even go down like that, so I keep my distance."

"You really have to find a better way to go about the situation, son. You really do. Y'all are siblings and all y'all have."

"Why I gotta find a better way to go about it? What would you rather me do, ma? You want me to go over there and put an ice pack on her face? You want me to tell her to go to couple's counseling? Hell naw! My only advice is to pop that nigga."

"I don't need you to do anything, Eastland." Emersyn appeared at the entryway of the kitchen, hood still over her head. East surveyed her sweats that were two sizes too big and her running shoes. In his head, her attire screamed *battered woman on the run.* He hated to see his once strong sister in that predicament.

"Come in and have a seat, Emmy. I'm gonna whip up something for us to eat."

"Ma, we not gon' pretend like y'all wasn't just in here talkin' bout me."

"Same shit I say to mommy, I don't mind saying in your face, Emersyn. Ain't shit changed."

"Alright, y'all, don't start that." Ms. Evelyn hated when her kids argued in her presence. They didn't know when to let up and often times they ended up saying hurtful things to each other that neither one could take back.

"It's him, ma. Judging a situation that he doesn't understand!" Emersyn shouted and East silently coached himself to remain calm out of respect for his mom.

"Yeah, it's time for me to go before I hurt your feelings." He finished his apple, discarded it in the trash, and kissed his mother's cheek. "Love you. I'll call you tomorrow." He then went to walk out the kitchen and stopped next to a fired-up Emersyn. "I love you, too, sis, and I'm still here."

Getting back in his car, East sighed before starting it up. Dealing with his sister often put him in a bad headspace. Sometimes he felt more at ease when she didn't come around, then he didn't have to deal with the reality that she wouldn't let him save her. It was a tough pill to swallow, but his hands were tied. Pulling off, he shook his thoughts free of Emersyn's drama. He had to figure out how he was going to pull off dinner and hopefully get Katori to let at least one wall down. He hoped that her spending time with Tima made her less hostile than she was earlier. Lord knows, he didn't have it in him to deal with anymore drama for the night.

Chapter 11

Katori awoke from what was supposed to be a twenty-minute cat nap, two hours later. She sat up straight on the couch and stretched her arms over her head. Feeling a tightness in her neck, she twisted from side to side to get the kinks out.

"It's been a minute since we had to squabble. Them muscles feeling it, huh?" Fatima came in from the kitchen with her wine glass in hand.

Katori chuckled. "Girl, a squabble would imply that I let a bitch gets some hits in. I was dogging that hoe. The only person that got a good hit in was the one who snuck me. Why you let me sleep so long?"

"You looked peaceful and after the today's events, you needed that rest. I took a little nap, too." Fatima sat down next to Katori and stared at her over the rim of her glass as she sipped the whine.

"What?" Katori let out, through a yawn.

"My cousin likes you."

"And I like money, what's your point?"

"Well, there's one thing you two have in common," Fatima pointed out. Katori rolled her eyes. "And there's that, y'all both have ugly attitudes at times. See, two for two already."

"Mmhmm. And now that you know who he is, you better not me talking about me to him. Remember, you my friend."

"Yes, your friend that wants to see you happy and in loveeeee."

"Been there, done that, got the pictures and memories to prove it."

"You loved Rob, but you weren't in love with him. That came from your own mouth, remember."

Katori didn't need to think about what Fatima said because it was the truth. While she loved Rob, she knew she wasn't in love with him. It was only after a year of living with him did she realize that fact. She loved being around him, but she didn't crave his presence when he was away. She felt protected by him, but she never felt safe enough to be vulnerable. In hindsight, those things may have also contributed to the reason she didn't want to have a baby with him.

"That's true, but you know what I mean."

"I do and as long as you're not closing yourself off to the possibility of falling in love then I'ma back off. For the record, Eastland is good people. He gon' tell you how he feels at any given moment, but he's a good guy. I'm not just saying that because we're family. It wouldn't hurt to go out to dinner or maybe brunch. Hell, you living in the man's condo."

"Temporarily."

"Tomato, tomahto."

Katori stood up from the couch and stretched her body. "Let me get ready to go. I'm gonna need you to help me look for a place soon."

"Or you can get one of them… umm, what them people called…" Fatima snapped her fingers, "oh, yeah, a realtor."

"A realtor is not in my budget. If it was, I wouldn't be asking you, smart ass." Katori threw a pillow from the couch at her, which she dodged.

"Okayyy," Fatima giggled. "I'll help you. Just know that I'm not going to more than five showings."

"Make it six, pleaseeeee."

"Ughh, alright. How you getting home?"

"I'm taking an Uber to East's condo."

Fatima smirked. "You want me to order it for you while you get your stuff together?"

"Yes, please. I know the longer I wait, the less cars will be available. Thanks, boo."

"Got you."

As soon as Katori walked away, Fatima texted East. He texted back that he was en route and would let her know when he was downstairs. Setting her phone back down,

Fatima prayed that Katori wouldn't be too mad about the set up. *She'll be grateful for the outcome,* she reasoned.

ME: I knew you were up to no good. Oooh, payback is a bitch.

Katori threatened Fatima through text once she made it downstairs and saw East standing in front of a black truck, on his phone. She should've known something was up by the way Tima all but forced her out of the apartment. Tima texted back that she would deal with whatever consequence just to see her best friend happy. Katori wasn't buying any of the cute shit, though. She still wasn't feeling East from earlier and the last thing she wanted to do was get into a battle of words with him as tired as she was.

Sucking her teeth, she pushed the door open and walked out onto the street. She was a few feet away when he lifted his head and met her eyes. Something in the look he gave her made her slow down her stride.

"Are you okay?" She asked once she was closer to him. She didn't know him well enough to read him, but she sensed something was off.

"I'm straight," he replied, dully and opened the door for her.

Katori's first mind was to decline but she lifted her leg up and climbed inside the truck. Making sure she was good,

East closed the door, hopped in the driver's side, and pulled off.

"You hungry?"

"I could eat. It's late though, and I don't want fast food."

"I got you," he assured her. "You wanna listen to music?"

"Nah, I got a lot on my head. I could use the silence to sort through my thoughts."

"Same."

Katori let the window down a little bit, taking in the night breeze, and letting the sound of the wind soothe her busy mind. This drive was different. Not in an awkward way, but it was the first time they'd been in the car alone without Tae in the backseat.

"Everything cool with, Tae?"

"Yeah. He's at our family's house for the weekend."

"Cool." East went quiet before speaking again. "Ay, about earlier."

Katori held her hand up. "No need to apologize. You said how you felt." She didn't want to rehash their spat.

"I wasn't about to apologize. I do wanna explain what I meant."

She cut her eye at him. "Are you serious?"

"Deadass. You want me to lie?"

"I don't want you to do anything." Feeling herself getting mad, she checked her tone. East had already made her come out of her body once, she didn't want to give him that power again.

"I see you don't like people being honest witchu. You can't handle it."

"No, I take honesty very well. Your delivery is what I took offense to."

"How was my delivery offensive? I didn't call you out your name or disrespect you."

"Yeah, but—."

"But what?"

"Nothing."

"Man, you ain't gotta be so tough, shorty. That shit ain't healthy. Letting yo guard down don't make you weak either, it makes you human."

She heard his words but didn't respond. No one outside of Fatima had ever called her out on her attitude or how she showed up. Katori knew she didn't always show herself friendly, but it was for good reason. Leaning her head up against the window, she closed her eyes and spoke how she truly felt.

"Eastland, I don't know how to react to you. I don't know how to take you. You killed someone in front of me, someone that once meant something to me, yet I find myself attracted to you. It's wrong, morally. Even after finding out the bullshit that Rob was doing right under my nose, it's still wrong."

"You plan on telling somebody that I killed ol' boy?"

Katori's eyes popped open, and she quickly turned to him. "What?! No, of course not."

"Why? And don't say no lame shit like, *you ain't no snitch.* You're a civilian, that shit don't apply to you."

"I don't have an answer for that."

"You do, but I respect that you don't wanna say it out loud, so I'll drop it. How about we just start with dinner? I ain't tryna get married tomorrow or nothing like that but I like yo vibe. We've already established that we met on fucked up terms, that's a moment in time that neither one of us can take back. All we can do is choose how we want to move forward. I'd like to get to know you and for you to get to know me. There's more than what meets the eye. If you feel like it's too much to ask, I'll fall back."

Katori contemplated her next move before responding. "I can do dinner."

East nodded and stopped the car. They'd been so engrossed in conversation, she didn't notice that they'd pulled up to the condo. "Come on, let's eat," he said, getting out of the car.

"Hold on, we're not going out?" Katori asked, confused, and still planted in her seat.

"Not tonight, I cooked." He reached for the door handle, and she leaned back.

"Cooked what?"

"Food, crazy girl." He laughed. "Come on and get out so you can see what I whipped up." He opened the door, and she got out slowly.

"Good evening," Paul spoke, and held the door open for them. He gave East a thumbs up on the low as they walked in.

Following behind East, Katori wondered what he had up his sleeve. "Eastland," she spoke in a soft tone.

"Wassup, girl."

"Can you cook?"

He pressed for the elevator and stepped back to stand next to her. "Nah, I followed a recipe online. I ain't gon' cap, at first, I was gonna have my mom's whip up something quick, but that didn't work out, so I went with my plan B. "You followed a recipe? What did you make?"

"Fix your face." He chuckled as they got on the elevator. "You look worried as hell."

"Shit, I am. You just admitted that you don't know how to cook, yet you made a meal."

"Hey," he shrugged, "I gotta start somewhere, right."

"And you want me to be the test dummy. Unbelievable."

Entering the condo, Katori picked up on the faint smell of garlic and tomato sauce. She headed straight for the kitchen to check he pots on the stove. In one pot there was spaghetti noodles and the other had meat and sauce. She breathed a little easy, thinking, spaghetti was an easy meal that didn't require many ingredients or much effort.

"How come you didn't mix everything together?"

"That's not how the recipe said to do it." East took of his coat and threw it on the couch. "Go wash your hands so we can eat."

"You wash yours, too. And hand me your coat so I can hang it up." He did as she requested and went over to the kitchen sink to wash his hands.

Katori hung both coats up in the hallway closet and disappeared to the back of the house. East was confident in the meal he'd prepared. He took his time and followed the recipe down to the letter. He even added the sugar, although he was sure his mother would lose her mind if she'd seen him do it. Remembering that he didn't get to do a taste test because he had to run out, he grabbed a spoon and put it in the spaghetti sauce. The sauce was savory and had a hint of sweetness. Different from the spaghetti he'd grown up on but good.

"You better not put that spoon back in that pot either," Katori scolded him as she reentered the kitchen. She'd traded her dress for a pair of sweatpants and a baby doll tee.

"Say I won't stick my finger in it." East held his finger over the pot with a smirk.

"You could and you'll be eating by your damn self, I'll tell you that much."

He laughed and tossed the spoon he used in the sink. "And let you miss out on the pleasure of getting to know me, nah. Sit down at the table, I'll make the plates."

Katori made sure to sit down in the chair that put him in her line of sight. She wanted to watch his every move to make sure he didn't do anything to her food. She was opening up to the idea of being more friendly, but that trust thing, not even close.

Chapter 12

"This is good," Katori complimented. She was down to her last two forkfuls and had she not had sweats on, she would've unbuttoned her pants. East had given her a hearty portion and she was stuffed.

"Yeah, I did my thing. Just call me Chef Boy Ar East." He rubbed his hands together and Katori bussed out laughing.

"You've been waiting for the opportunity to say that, huh?"

"Yeah." He laughed along with her. "How does your face feel?"

"What you mean? Is there something on it?" She picked up her napkin and wiped around

her mouth.

"Nah, you good. I only asked because you're smiling. It's

the first time I've seen you do that. I wanna know how it feels."

"It feels good because I'm not forcing it. I know I may give off a vibe like I'm unhappy or I don't like people but I'm good, I'm just always in plan mode. Feels like I'm always tryna figure something out, ya know. Like I can't just be."

"Maybe it's not because you can't, maybe you just won't allow yourself to."

Katori cast her eyes downward and used her fork to play with the remaining spaghetti on her plate. "My mother died a few years back and it's just been me and Tae since then as far as family goes. When we moved in with Rob, I was hesitant because in the back of my mind, I knew it would change our relationship dynamic. I still moved forward because I knew Tae needed stability. I never knew how much I changed after my mom's death. I smiled a lot less, and if I'm honest with myself I kind of detached myself from people outside of my circle. A circle that only consisted of Tae, Tima, and Rob. The reason why you calling me out set me off is because you were right."

"How do you feel right here, right now?"

Katori stopped fiddling with the fork and put her head up. "Vulnerable."

"I can meet you where you are, so you don't have to be there by yourself."

"Okay." She dropped her fork, and put her arms on the table, giving him her full attention.

"I have a sister who I love with all my heart and would

lay down my life for. I'm in control of everything in my life. I have money at my disposal, a team that moves when I say, but even with my power and influence, I can't convince my sister to leave her abusive relationship. I walked into my mama's house tonight and seen her for the first time in a while. She had two black eyes, and she was smaller than when I'd seen her last. Her mentality hasn't changed and her stance on staying hasn't either. I think about it daily and though I hate to admit it, her relationship with her nigga has changed our relationship completely."

"And what do you suppose she do?"

"Shit, leave that nigga. All she gotta do is leave and I'll handle the rest."

"Though it's easy to suggest, it's not always easy to do. It's really a mental thing."

"You sound like my mama."

"It's true."

Taking a bite of his food, he sipped his drink. "You know from experience?"

"Oh, no, that's one thing I don't play about. A nigga put his hands on me, I'll be on an episode of Snapped."

"That's the type of energy I want my sister to have."

"And she probably has it in her, but only she'll know when enough is enough and she's ready to leave. You just need to make sure that when she's ready, you're willing to put you aside to be there as her brother. You finished with that?" She pointed to his plate.

"Yeah." Taking the plate from him, she went into the kitchen.

The night was turning out better than East thought it would. He'd gotten Katori to express herself without being defensive which in turn made him want to open up as well. Still, he didn't know what would come from tonight. And as he thought about it, he figured it was best not to set an expectation. The last thing he wanted was for her to crawl back up in a shell. The lyrics to Drake & 21 Savage "Treacherous Twins" ring out from her phone that sat on the table.

"Can you bring me my phone and put it on speaker, that's Tae." Picking up the phone, he answered it and sat it on the sink where she was washing the dishes. The crying in the background put the both of them on alert.

"Tae, what's going on, who's crying?"

"Can you come scoop me and Kita from Aunt Gloria's? She just got into it with her people and these mother.... Man, just come here and I'll explain."

"Alright, I'm coming."

Hanging up her phone, Katori rushed out of the kitchen and to the bedroom. She threw on her sneakers and rummaged through her suitcase to find her brass knuckles. Locating them inside her makeup bag, she grabbed her coat, and slid the brass knuckles in the pocket.

"What's going on with yo' people?" East questioned as she breezed past him.

"I don't know, but I'm sure as hell bout to find. Bitches

better pray that not a single curl on my brother's head is touched."

Katori would take it to the furthest extent behind Dontae. Shaking his head, East went to grab his coat. He didn't know what he was about to get himself into but made sure that his gun was locked and loaded. Katori didn't need to ask for his protection, she already had it.

PULLING up to her Aunt Gloria's house, Katori hopped out of the car like her ass was on fire. "Where Tae at?" She asked her cousins, who she recognized sitting outside in the courtyard.

"Wassup, Tori. He's in the house with Kita and my mama," her cousin, Jonah answered.

"Thanks," she replied and continued straight ahead, into her aunt's building. She didn't have time to kick it. Katori needed to lay eyes on her brother.

East stepped out of the car, walked around to the passenger side, and leaned up against it with his gun in hand. With the way Katori was moving, he was on guard and ready to pop at any minute. Even though they were at her people's house, he wasn't taking any chances. He could tell she wasn't either. Before he let her put herself in a position that could potentially land her in jail, he would let his Ruger do the talking and gladly pay for the cleanup bill.

A few minutes later, Katori stormed out of the building,

with a fuming Tae and a distraught Kita holding onto his arm for dear life. Before they could reach the car, Kita bent over, holding her stomach with pain etched across her face. Thinking she was in pain from the fight, Tae moved his arm so that he was holding her around her waist. As they got closer to the car, Kita was damn near dragging the ground, in tears. Seeing the state Kita was in, East pushed off the car and walked closer to them.

"I think something is wrong. I'm in so much pain," Kita cried out as she gripped her stomach. The cramping she experienced was worse than her normal period cramps. It was so intense that she began to panic and hyperventilate.

"Kita, it's gonna be okay. I got you." Poor Tae was doing everything he could to get her to the car quickly. Katori went to the other side of Kita to help Tae keep her up.

When East was close enough to see Kita's bruised face, his blood boiled. Although the young lady wasn't his responsibility, her people didn't have to do her like that. Seeing that Tae was doing his best to maintain his composure along with his sister, East asked their permission to pick Kita up. They all agreed, and East scooped her up bridal style, carried her to the car, and placed her inside gently.

Before he could close the door, Kita let out a scream so loud it shook Tae to his core. Jumping in the car, the four of them peeled off and headed to the hospital.

Knowing Kita wasn't in a position to talk, Katori began interrogating Tae on what all took place. "What the hell happened, Tae?!"

"Tori, stop hollering at me! You've been doing that since you pulled up."

"Dontae, if you don't start talking, I know something."

"I can't talk with you yellin'."

Katori took a deep breath, mustering up all the patience she had left. With Kita in the backseat, laid out in Tae's lap, it was hard for her to remain levelheaded in her questioning. His stalling wasn't making the situation any better.

"Everybody chill," East intervened. "What happened, Tae?" He went with the calm approach, in an effort to ease the tension.

"And don't leave shit out!" Katori added. East grilled her and she rolled her eyes.

"Kita decided that she wanted to be upfront with her aunt about the pregnancy. She said being secretive was adding to her stress and she just wanted to have a clear conscience. She let her know that we had a slip up and explained that she understood the consequences of her actions."

"Tae, please speed the hell up to the part where you explain to me why her eye is black, her face is swollen, and her damn nose is bleeding."

"Dang, Tori I'm getting to that part," Tae expressed, frustrated. Katori glanced back at Kita who was now rocking back and forth with her eyes closed. "Kita said she told her aunt that she wasn't ready for a baby and asked if she could just give consent for her to get the abortion. Her aunt flew off the handle, calling Kita all types of hoes before jumping on her, along with her cousins."

Katori spun around so fast and all but stood up in the seat. "You mean to tell me all them goddamn people jumped on this girl after said she was pregnant?" Katori summed up what he'd explained as if the story would change. Tae nodded and she turned back around. "Say no more."

East listened to the story as he drove and knew Katori was prepared to take matters into her own hands. Little did she know, as soon as they got to the hospital, he was going to hit up Trill and do some digging. Once again, he had made her problems, his problems.

Chapter 13

Arriving at the hospital, Tae was out of the car as soon as East put it in park. He went to help Kita out, and Katori was the first one to notice blood on the seat. Kita happened to turn around and when she saw it, her eyes got big. She'd felt something wet between her legs during the ride, but the pain in her stomach had her full attention.

"It's okay, Kita. Come on, let's go inside so they can check you out," Katori spoke, grabbing hold of her hand.

"I'm…I'm sorry," Kita said to East before dropping her head.

"You good, shorty. Don't even worry bout it. I'm gonna be right here waiting for y'all, Katori."

Tae looked at his sister with concerned filled eyes as they walked inside of the emergency room. Katori had no words to console him. She halfway wanted to leave Tae in the hospital with Kita and have East take her to Kita's house. She wanted to do damage with the brass knuckles.

"Oh, goodness, here, let me help," one of the hospital personnel at the front desk offered. She got up from behind the desk and grabbed a wheelchair for Kita.

"She was jumped and she's pregnant. I believe she's miscarrying." Katori spoke on Kita's behalf.

The woman sprang into action, paging for someone to come to the ER from the labor and delivery unit. With everything happening so fast, Tae didn't have a chance to kiss Kita like he wanted to before they wheeled her to the back. With Katori being the only adult present to speak on Kita's behalf, she gave Kita's name and had Tae give any other important information needed. When the woman asked about a parent, Tae was tight lipped but, Katori made him give the aunt's name.

"I don't know her phone number. You have to get that from Kita," Tae let the woman know.

She nodded and assured them that she'd have an update as soon as she knew something about Kita's condition. "You two can have a seat in the waiting room."

Katori pulled Tae over to the waiting area and made him sit down.

"Why we had to tell her about Kita's aunt? You could've said you were her legal guardian."

"Come on Tae, you know there was no way around that. By law them people need to know who her guardian is."

"For what? Ain't like she gon' do shit when she gets here.

If she even comes. That lady hates her own blood and the crazy thing about it is, Kita don't know why. They ain't have to jump my girl like that, Tori. They ain't have to do her like that." The emotion in Tae's voice made Katori shed a tear. Her brother was hurting, and his pain was her pain.

"Dontae, hear me when I tell you, I'm going to take care of it."

Tae nodded and put his head in his hands. Although they'd agreed that Kita wouldn't go through with the pregnancy, Tae was sure that the miscarriage would put her in one of those depressive states she often fell into. While he was always by her side to coach her through them, there was but so much that Kita would allow him to do. He hated knowing that after all of this, she would still have to return back to the home where she experienced the trauma.

About an hour later, the same woman who'd taken Kita's information came into the waiting room to find them, along with a nurse.

Tae was the first one to jump up from his seat. "Is she okay?"

"Yes," the nurse spoke. "She did suffer a miscarriage. Thankfully, she has no broken bones or anything from the fight. As you both saw, her face is pretty bruised up, but she'll heal. We tried to contact her guardian but received no answer. Maybe one of you can try. We just want to inform the aunt that we'll be keeping Kita for overnight observation."

"Ummm, she's, my girlfriend. Do you think I can go back and see her?" Tae asked.

"Sure. You have about an hour before visiting hours are over. I'll take you to her."

"I'll wait right here for you," Katori said. Once Tae and the nurse were out of earshot, the woman from the front desk spoke.

"Hey, I could get in trouble for this, but I wanted to let you know that I did get in touch with her guardian."

"Really?"

"Yeah. She told me that she wasn't coming down to the hospital and for us to deal with the situation as we saw fit."

"Are you serious?" Katori was disgusted.

"Yeah. I was going to try again. I hate to call CPS for minors. I always feel like I'm aiding in tossing the kids in the system."

Katori appreciated the woman looking out and told her so. "I know this may be a lot to ask and I'll understand if you told me no, but do you think you can note that you tried to call again, and her aunt gave me permission to take her home?" Katori knew it was a long shot, but she had to try something.

"Ma'am, I'm sorry, I wish I could, but I don't wanna lose my job."

"I get it. Thanks anyway."

Feeling defeated, Katori walked off towards the exit. She needed fresh air. Stepping outside, she sucked in a deep breath and let it out. She was one incident away from losing it, and seeing as she had no choice but to keep it together, she needed to regroup in order to make a sound decision.

WATCHING KATORI, Tae, and Kita disappear behind the double doors of the ER, East couldn't believe his night. He had seen and done a lot in his life but never had he witnessed the shit he saw tonight. Seeing the blood in his backseat, coupled with the horror and embarrassment on Kita's face, he became more inclined to handle the situation with her family on her behalf. As he sat in the car waiting, he put a call in to Trill.

"**Yo,**" Trill's voice came through the phone.

"**Mannn,**" Eastland let out, sighing deeply. "**I need you to get some information for me.**"

"**Aight, give me a name and I'll get right on it.**"

"**I'll have it for you in a minute. I just need you on standby.**"

"**On standby to get the information, or on standby ready to get in the field?**"

"**You know, for someone who's out the game, this is the second time you've referenced getting your hands dirty. Is there something I need to know?**"

"**Nah, man, I'm out.**"

"**Aight.**"

"**What you got going on, though?**"

East looked out the window and shook his head. "**I'm up**

here at the hospital with Katori, her brother, and his girl. Tae's girl got into it with her people, and they jumped her. She pregnant so they had to get her checked out and shit."

"Mann, you fucking with shorty like that?" Trill asked, referring to Katori. East didn't answer the question and Trill took it as him not wanting to express how he felt so he left it alone. What Trill did know was that he'd never seen his boy go to the lengths he'd gone for Katori for any woman. If subtly forcing her and her brother into his condo wasn't some Lifetime movie shit, then he didn't know what was.

East's eyes focused on the ER doors where he spotted Katori searching the parking lot. Assuming she was looking for him, he blew the horn and watched her make her way over to the car.

"Ay, let me hit you back," East told Trill before ending the call. He popped the locks, allowing Katori to get in. He noted that even with the worry line creasing her forehead, she was still as beautiful as the day he forced his way into her life. "What they say?"

"She had a miscarriage."

"Damn," he whispered. "That's fucked up."

"What's even more fucked up is that they reached out to the aunt to inform her of what's going on, and this bitch told them to handle it."

"Damn, sometimes it be yo own family."

"I swear when I see this bitch, I'm doing her so dirty. Did you see her damn face?"

"Let me handle it, Katori."

"No, you've handled enough. This is all me." Katori felt like she'd gone from hostage to burden in the last week, and she wasn't feeling that. In the last week alone she'd been thrown curveball after curveball and at this point, she felt like she wanted to throw in the towel.

"Why?!" She yelled out loud to no one in particular, throwing her head back on the headrest.

"Huh?" Her outburst and the look on of defeat on her face rubbed East the wrong way. He didn't do defeat and he wasn't about to let her concede to it in his presence. "Ay, chin up, beautiful. This shit ain't over, not by a long shot." She kept her head back with her eyes closed. "Are they keeping her?"

"Yes, just for observation. I don't know what's gonna happen tomorrow when they go to discharge her."

"You sure she don't have any other family that can come get her?"

"I don't know. I gotta ask Tae. He's in there visiting with her. I know she's not gonna wanna go back to her bitch ass aunt's house."

"I'm sure we'll figure something out that'll ease your mind and put Kita in a better position."

"I hope so." Katori couldn't let Kita go back home after that trauma. Something had to give.

Chapter 14

Back inside the hospital, Tae watched Kita sleep peacefully after the nurse administered her pain medication. He couldn't help but to think that everything was his fault. Had he not moved so careless, they could've avoided this. Kita opened her eyes and turned towards him.

"Hey," she spoke, and tried to muster up a smile, that didn't meet her eyes.

"Hey." He scooted his chair up so that was next to the bed. "How you feeling?"

"My stomach is cramping, and my face is a little sore. My side hurts a little, too."

"I'm sorry, Kita."

"What you sorry for? You didn't put me in this hospital bed."

"I know but—."

"No, Tae, don't blame yourself for some fucked up shit my family did. Them people are evil. You know, laying in that room, getting my baby sucked out of me, all I could think about was dying."

"Kita, don't say no shit like that, man."

"No, really, if I died, I'm sure they wouldn't even care."

"I'm going to talk to Katori."

"Talk to me about what?" Katori questioned, entering the hospital room. She'd sat in silence with East long enough and wanted to see Kita before visiting hours were over. "Talk to me about what?" She repeated, waiting for either one of them to speak up.

"Ummm, I was just wondering where Kita going after this?"

"I'm not sure. It's something I'm trying to figure out now. Do you have any other family members Kita?"

"I have an older cousin who lives in Brooklyn. I lived with her before moving in with my aunt. Well, she stayed with me and my mom in our apartment. When my mother passed, my aunt came and took me. Golden was only twenty-one at the time and even though she could take care of me, with her felony record, she wanted to stay out of the courts with my aunt."

"Are you still in contact with her?"

"No," Kita replied, sadly. "My aunt made me delete her number a while ago. According to her, Golden is a bad influence on me. The real reason was because Golden told her the same thing you told her; she was gonna beat her ass if she kept treating me wrong. I think I still have her on Facebook."

"Send her a message and let her know you're here."

"Okay."

"Come out here for a second, Tae." Tae walked out with Katori and stood outside the door. "I know what you were getting at back there and I thought about it, too, but I can't have Kita living with us."

"I figured that and I get it. I just wanna make sure she's safe."

"Same."

"Ay, y'all good?" They both turned to find East walking in their direction.

"How'd you get up here?"

"Same way you did, I took the elevator. Any update on her people?"

"She's reaching out to a cousin on Facebook," Katori answered.

"Thanks for helping us get here, man," Tae said to East. "I'm gonna get the blood out your car, too."

"I took care of it." Tae dapped East up. The announcement for the ending of visiting hours came over the loudspeaker. "I'm gonna go back in and see wassup."

"Alright." Katori waited until the door to the room was closed before speaking to East. "Hey, I just wanna say thank you for bringing us here and staying. I still don't know why you're moving on my behalf in such a way, but I appreciate it."

"I'd be lying if I said I knew. I'm here, though." East was acting out of the kindness of his heart and secretly, he felt like he owed it to her.

"I'd like to show my appreciation by whipping you up a meal."

"You…cook for me?" East pointed to himself.

"That's what I said. What, you don't think I can cook?"

"I'm saying, I'ma be honest with you and tell you if yo food ain't hittin'."

"Boy, please. You follow one spaghetti recipe and now you Top Chef." They both laughed "Trust me, my cooking will have you coming back for seconds."

East's mind immediately went to a nasty place, and he thought about giving her a second and third rounds of dick. Tae peeking out of the room, pulled his mind from the gutter.

"Her cousin is coming in the morning to sign her out."

"Perfect. Let me go say goodnight."

"Let me holla at you, Tae." East led him over to the elevators to talk. "How you holding up?"

Tae scratched his head and sighed. "I'm doing what I can to make sure she straight. I really wanna spazz out but I know she wouldn't want me to. Kita is really a dope person, and she wants the best for everyone around her. It's crazy that her own family treat her the way they do. Jealous ass bitches. Her aunt don't even have the decency to make sure she has the necessities. If it wasn't for Katori boosting, she would be wearing them same hand me downs."

"Yo sister boosts clothes?"

Tae had been so busy venting that he had slipped up and mentioned Katori's side hustle on accident. He knew it wasn't something that she told East because she was private with that information. The only people who knew how Katori got down were her clients and they were a select few. Having already put it out there, Tae knew he couldn't take it back, but he wasn't going to confirm by repeating it.

"I don't know what you talkin' bout."

East smiled, respecting that Tae was protective of his sister. "Shit, me neither. I need something from you, though."

"Wassup?"

"I need the names of the people who jumped ya girl. I know she said she don't—."

"Tracey, Brittany, and Raneka Blackwell. Raneka is Kita's aunt and the other two are the cousins. Kita will just have to understand. I don't want them killed, just fucked over."

"Chill on the k word, kidd. We got ears everywhere," he said.

"Damn, my bad. I'm kinda all over the place."

"You good. Always make sure you think before you talk. No matter the situation you're in, think first." East gave him some quick game.

Tae nodded, taking the advice. "I appreciate what you're doing for my sister. And I'm not talking about putting us up in the condo either. You took her out of a situation that she needed to fully walk away from. She may not agree with the way it was done, but some things are necessary for the greater good."

Tae put his hand out for East to dap and he did. The sixteen-year-old had given him food for thought, and further proved that his plan to pursue Katori was for good reason.

AFTER MAKING sure Tae and Katori got back home, East headed to his place. He'd been on the move the last couple days and hadn't seen his bed. He thought about calling up Yanna for a night cap but quickly nixed the thought. He knew she'd end up over his crib with her spennanight bag and he wasn't in that mood. The one person he wouldn't mind being cuddled next to wasn't ready for all that, so he opted to call it a night alone.

No sooner than he pulled onto his street, his trap phone rang. East didn't get calls late at night from the trap unless something was wrong, so even though he wanted to decline the call, he answered.

"**Yo.**"

"**Boss man, we gotta shut down shop.**"

East just knew he was hearing things. "**Fuck you mean we gotta shut down shop, Nike?**" East was exhausted and with the day he had, he owed himself a few hours of sleep. However, the universe just wouldn't let him be great. "**Goddamn!**"

"**Ay, boss man, you good?**"

"Yeah, I'm good, regular shit. What kind of fuckin' question is that to ask, dummy?! You calling talkin' bout shutting down shop then gon'... you know what, I'm on my way. When I get there make sure you're as far away from me as possible. I just might smack the shit outta you just because. Clear my line for I get mad, Nike."

East disconnected the call, pissed at his soldier's stupidity. There were only two reasons for ever shutting down shop; if the spot was hot or if it was robbed. To East's knowledge, he wasn't on the cop's radar so that only left option number two. East didn't sit that high to think that niggas wouldn't try him, it came with the occupation. The problem was, niggas wasn't ready to die about they shit if it came down to it, and unfortunately for them, East was ready to kill.

Bussing a U-turn in the middle of his street, East mashed the gas on his truck, en route to the trap. In his haste to get there, he ignored the call that came in from his mother. When she called again, he answered.

"Ma, I have something important to handle, I can't stay on the phone long. You alright?"

"Yeah, I'm okay, but something is up with Emersyn."

"We already know what's up with Emmy. That's not something I can deal with right now."

"No, Eastland, there's something deeper going on. I know my child."

East blew out an exasperated breath, tired of doing the same song and dance with his mother. With what he'd just learned about his trap, the last thing he wanted to do was be bothered with a situation he had no control over. He hated that his mother was stressing about it, but Emersyn was her child, and it didn't matter how many times she went back to her situation, their mother was gonna be there.

"**What do you think is going on, ma? Cause all I seen was the same bruises that I've seen in the past.**"

"**I don't know, Eastland. She keeps walking by the windows and checking outside. I don't know if she's waiting for something to happen or what.**" Her statement made him a little more alert.

"**Did she drive herself there?**"

"**No. She said she took an Uber.**" Uneasy, he asked her to put Emersyn on the phone. "**That'll just make it more obvious that I'm worrying. You know y'all don't like it when I worry.**"

"**Yet you called me. Ma, put her on the phone.**"

"**Hey, watch your tone. You keep that street shit in the street and handle me according to my title.**"

"**Aight, ma. Can you go get her for me, please.**"

"**Hold on.**" The call went silent, and East connected the phone to the car.

"**Hello,**" Emersyn's voice came through the phone, and he immediately picked up on what his mother was talking about.

East cleared his throat to make sure his sister heard him loud and clear when he spoke. "**I need you listening cause I'm only gonna say this once. What you do with your life** is your business until you make it mine. That said, if that nigga come to my mama house looking for you, I'm gonna make sure he has a close casket. Stay silent if you understand me." When Emersyn said nothing, East took that as a sign that they were on the same page. "I'm glad we we're on the same page, sis." He hung up the phone and turned his ringer off. If the night called for him to get active, he didn't need any interruptions.

Chapter 15

Pulling up to the trap, in the Bronx that Nike worked out of, East hopped out on a mission to find out who in their right mind wanted to play with their life on a nice Fall evening. He had a one-track mind as he nodded at each one of his soldiers on the way inside.

"Where Fabo?" East asked, in search of his second in command.

Fabo had taken Trill's spot after he got jammed up. He was one unhinged ass dude, and the soldiers were scared of him, although no one admitted it out loud. While Fabo was unstable, he was loyal to the soil. He ran a tight ship and East knew if someone had robbed his spot, they were as good as dead. Fabo didn't play fair when it came down to putting in work.

"Aye yo' you," Fabo called out to East from the back of the

trap, sounding like Lyfe Jennings. It was his signature call to East.

Fabo was a dark skinned, dread head who stood at six foot five, and kept his signature blond and black dreads pulled up in lazy bun. He was handsome and the women always flocked his way, but they never stayed too long. They always found him hard to figure out. Funny how it was the mystery that pulled them in, and at the same time pushed them away. Though Fabo was known to be entertaining, he had a mean streak and no tolerance for bullshit. In his world you were either an associate or an enemy; he didn't do friends.

"Man, what the fuck happened?" East asked, making his way through the house towards the back where he heard Fabo.

"Nike called you right?" Fabo asked, calmly. East nodded, knowing Fabo was going to follow up with something ignorant. "Well, the lil nigga called me, too."

"And what they hell that supposed to mean, nigga?" East stepped back and looked at Fabo crazy while Fabo did the same.

"I'm just saying if he called you, right… and he called me, right, how the hell I'm supposed to know what happened if I just got here?"

"Nigga, I ain't know you just got here. I ain't clockin' yo moves."

"Yeah, well, somebody clockin' the moves of the people in this bitch cause how the fuck we get robbed on my day off?"

Fabo pointed up to the ceiling, in the corner, and East could see that the floorboard to the attic where they stashed work and money had been ripped out. That nobody count October was starting to sound like a joke.

"Where that nigga Nike at, anyway? I ain't see him outside when I came."

"Ion know but the shit ain't sitting well with me that his ass ain't here. How you gon' call a parlay and not be here to conduct it."

"A parlay? Fuck is you talkin' bout, Fabo?"

"You ain't seen John Wick 4?"

"Mannn, come on so we can run these cameras. You talkin' bout a goddamn parlay. I'm tired as fuck and ready to get my ass home."

"Same, nigga." Fabo took out his phone and pulled up the security app he used to monitor the cameras in the trap that only he and East knew about.

He fast forwarded what was recording for the day up until an hour before he remembered getting the call from Nike. Holding the phone up so that it was easy for East to see, the two watched the video in silence. They watched as two soldiers, MoMoney and Roger worked inside, while Nike, Blaze, Don, and Reggie posted up outside. Everything appeared normal until they saw two hooded men walk up on the soldiers outside.

"Look at his bitch ass," Fabo let out, watching Nike put his hands up as soon as one of the hooded men pulled their guns.

Nike, Blaze, Don, and Reggie were all forced into the house at gun point. Fabo hit another square, that prompted the camera inside the house where MoMoney and Roger sat to pop up. As if he'd been coached on where to go, one of the gunmen headed for the back room. Fabo gripped his phone tight as he watched the whole robbery take place.

"These niggas came up in this bitch and was gone in 300 seconds. Two niggas, two guns, versus six of our people with guns. You wanna do the math or let me do it?"

"Go head, Fabo," East said, pinching the bridge of his nose.

"Four scary niggas outside, plus two ducks inside, equals six dead bitches. How you wanna play it?"

"Shut the house down, call a meeting with the six and take care of it."

"Aight. That give me time to go get my shit together. I'll give the video another good look, see if anything stands out about the thieves."

"Aight, man. Try not to kill everybody. I don't want too many new niggas in the spot."

"You told me to handle it, so I gotta see it through my boy." East shook his head and dapped Fabo up. He'd had half the answers, and he knew Fabo would get the rest. He'd let Fabo deal with the soldiers, while he dealt with the culprits personally.

THE NEXT MORNING, Katori woke up early so that she and Tae could head over to the hospital to see about Kita. Katori wanted to make sure that her cousin came through like she said she would. Kita was in a fragile state and Katori knew she needed to be surrounded by love and people that cared about her. Getting out of bed, she went to see if Tae was up. Peeking inside the room, she found the bed empty, but the sheets were ruffled as if he had slept in the bed.

Continuing on to the living room, she found him fast asleep on the couch with his phone next to him. By the way he slept curled up on the phone, she knew Kita was on the other end. Picking the phone up, just as expected, Kita was on the other end of the FaceTime call, only she was up.

"**Good morning,**" Katori whispered, walking out of the living room.

"**Morning,**" Kita replied.

"**How you feeling?**"

"**Ehhh, I'm alright, I guess. Just ready to get outta here and out of this hospital gown.**"

"**I bet. I'm gonna bring you something to throw on. We'll be there in a few. Did your cousin say what time she was coming?**" Kita went silent and Katori was hoping she didn't say the cousin had changed her mind. "**She's still coming, right.**"

"**Oh, yeah. My bad, I was checking her text to see what time she said. She'll be here at twelve.**"

"**Okay, good. We'll be there before then. You want anything to eat?**"

"Oooh, can you bring me a bacon, egg, and cheese, please."

"I got you."

"Okay. And Katori..."

"Wassup, boo?"

"Thank you. I can't thank you enough."

"Just wrap it up and we're good." Kita covered her eyes with her hands to hide her face. "Mmmhmm." Katori laughed lightly and tapped Tae to wake him up. "Here, bro. I'm about to get ready, get up." She handed him the phone and walked back to the room.

Gathering her stuff for the shower, she noticed she was down to one outfit and two pairs of underwear. With all that had been going on, she hadn't gotten a chance to return to Rob's apartment to retrieve the rest of her belongings. After the brawl that happened at the funeral, she was sure that Patrice wasn't gonna give her access to do so. She hated to count it as a loss, but she knew she had to chalk it up to just that.

Stripping out of her clothes, Katori checked her phone and saw that she had a missed text from East. Checking the time stamp on the message, it was easy to see why she had missed it. He'd texted her at three in the morning. Katori had been on her fourth dream by that time. Unlocking her phone, she opened up the message to read it.

Eastland: I know by the time you get to read this message your face gon' be all scrunched up, mad because I texted you so late. My bad in advance. You were on my

mind, and I wanted to hit you before I went to sleep. I can't getcho mean ass off my mind. And don't go getting in your feelings about me calling you mean. I like you that way. YOU DON'T NEED TO BE FRIENDLY WITH NO NIGGAS BUT ME MOVING FORWARD. I'm snatching you up and ion care if you ready, get ready. But nah, you were on my mind, and I said all this to say, goodnight. LMAO hit me when you get this message.

Katori laughed, reading the message again. It was crazy that East couldn't get her off his mind because he'd consumed her thoughts all night. She even dreamed about him, and it was one nasty dream that she wanted to keep to herself. Texting him back, she let him know that she was going back to the hospital with Tae and asked if he would be available for dinner later. He responded back immediately.

Eastland: It's a date. And you can't back out either.

Me: What you wanna eat?

Eastland: Besides you, umm, surprise me.

Katori's clit thumped at his sexual innuendo. She didn't know what to respond back because apart of her wanting to engage in the flirtation. Thinking it over, she kept the message short, sweet, and PG-13.

Me: Be here by 9.

Eastland: Yo scary ass, lol. See you then.

Blushing hard, Katori headed for the shower. Eastland was breaking her down.

Chapter 16

By the time East woke back up to start his day it was three o' clock in the afternoon. He didn't mean to sleep so long but it was clear that his body needed the rest, his mind, too. Sitting up in bed, he stretched and reached for his phones. The trap phone had no notifications, but his personal phone had one missed call from Yanna, a text message from his mother, and a text message from Katori. He opened the message from his mother first. She'd asked him to stop by her house before he started his day. He replied that he would and moved onto the message from Katori.

In her message, she gave a quick update on Kita and confirmed their dinner date. Letting her know that the date was still a go, he sent his well wishes to Kita. While the subject was fresh on his brain, he texted Trill the names Tae had given him. With Kita leaving the hospital, he wanted to put Martinique and her crew up on game.

Me: Raneka, Tracey, and Brittany Blackwell are the names of the people I want you to get me information on. You don't have to do a deep dive, I just wanna know where they chill at and where they work at.

Trill: I'm on it.

Exiting out of the text threads, East dialed Yanna's number. The phone rang once before going to voicemail. Knowing she'd call back once she seen his missed call, East went into the bathroom to relieve himself. Finishing up, he jumped in the shower. Reaching into his shower caddy to grab his body wash, he noticed a hair tie that was underneath the bodywash bottle.

It was clear that it was intentionally put there and the only person he entertained on that level was Yanna. Chuckling to himself, at the strategic placement of the hair tie, East slid the shower door open and tossed it in the trash. Crazy how it would pop up after he'd basically told Katori she was his. Knowing he meant everything he said, he had no problem cutting Yanna off if Katori was open to the idea of seeing him.

Rinsing off, he stepped out of the shower and wrapped a towel around the bottom half of his body. Throwing on a pair of Chromeheart jeans, t-shirt, and Chromeheart hoodie, he slid his watch on his wrist and hit his neck with a few sprays of Versace Eros cologne. Grabbing his wallet, car keys, and phones, he headed out the door. His first stop was to see his mother. Part of him hoped that Emersyn wasn't still at the house. He wasn't feeling the fact that her presence seemed to have his mother on edge. Pulling out of his parking spot and onto the street, his phone rang. It was Yanna returning his call.

"Wassup, Yanna."

"Nothing much, busy as ever."

"Better to be busy and paid than still and broke, I always tell you that."

"Yeah, I know. I wanted to reach out and let you know I found the perfect two-bedroom apartment for you. It's on the Upper Westside in Manhattan. Nice area, low crime rate. There's a lot of college students in the area. You wanna come out to see it? They got a nice king size bed in the master bedroom that we can see about. It'll be like old times."

The offer sounded tempting, but East knew what he wanted. **"I'm gonna pass. Can you send me the link to my phone for the place that way I can do a virtual tour."** East hadn't told Yanna the place wasn't for him, and she didn't ask.

"Yeah, sure. I'll send it right over and you can let me know what you think."

"Aight, cool. Thanks."

"You got it." She hung up quickly.

He hoped that Yanna would play it cool for the sake of their business relationship and friendship once she found out he was involved with someone. Thinking for a moment, East bust out laughing. With the kind of dick he was breaking Yanna off with, he knew their relationship wouldn't be the same. Something in him felt like Katori was worth making the change from available dick to exclusive dick. Tonight's dinner would determine that.

"MA, WHERE YOU AT?" East yelled out as he entered his mother's house. Closing the door behind him, his eyes searched the living room for Emersyn. A part of him wanted her to still be somewhere in the house. Him seeing her two days in a row would've been a record for her.

"I'm back here in the laundry room, Eastland. Quit yelling through the house like you don't have no sense," his mother yelled back, and he headed for the laundry room.

"How you gon' tell me to stop yelling but yell back at me."

"Cause this my house and I'm the mama, and I can do that." She dumped a load of white towels into the wash and started it. Eastland bear hugged her from behind, almost making her lose her balance. "Boy, you make me fall I'm gon' kick yo ass." She laughed and turned so that she could hug her son back. "What's wrong?"

East hugged her tight and kissed her cheek before pulling back. "Nothing, I just love you, mama."

"I love you, too. You spoke to your sister?"

Sucking his teeth, he leaned up against the doorframe. "How come you never ask if my sister spoke to me?"

"Okay, has your sister spoke to you?"

"Nah. You know she don't fuck with me like that. I still love her, though. Where she at anyway?"

"Probably in the room. On top of being antsy, she's been sleeping a lot, so I've been letting her be. I think things may be different this time. She hasn't stayed the night here in a while and she did last night."

East just nodded. He wanted things to be different, but he wouldn't get his hopes up. "Ay, ma."

"Yo?" She answered back, being funny.

East chuckled. "You a trip. Do you think a relationship can blossom out of tragedy?"

"What kind of tragedy?"

"Uhhh, let's say man meets woman, kills woman's boyfriend, falls for woman." His mother stared up at him and squinted her eyes.

"Boy, who you kill?" Ms. Evelyn knew the son she raised, and she prayed for him daily, sometimes twice a day.

"I plead the fifth," he responded.

"Right. It's best I don't know. Back to your scenario." She used air quotes and rolled her eyes. "I think anything is possible. At the same time, said killer needs to understand that he needs to pursue the relationship on the woman's terms. The situation is fragile, and he should treat it as such."

Nodding his understanding, he posed another question. "Can you see me in a relationship?"

"Yep, I see you married with at least one child, too. Your wife is headstrong, independent, and she don't take no shit. At the same time, her heart is gold, and her love feels and looks like security and peace. She protects your heart and prays for the people around you as a way to safeguard you. She's basically a female you. When you find the one, you'll know it."

Hearing her describe some of the qualities he saw in Katori made him smile. First there was confirmation from Tae and now his mother. He was two for two.

"Thanks, ma." He went to hug her, and his phone went off. "Hold on one second, lady." He answered the call on speakerphone.

"Aye, yo', you. Where you at?"

"I'm at ma's crib. Slide on me."

"Bet."

"Don't you think you should tell me who's sliding up to my crib?" His mother asked, imitating his slang.

"That's Fabo, ma. He won't be here for long."

"That's the crazy, dread head, right."

"Yeah." East cracked up.

"Meet that crazy nigga right in the living room. He's a sweetheart, but something is a little off about that boy. I'll be in my room."

"Aight, ma. I got you."

East headed for the living room to wait for Fabo and found his sister sitting at the breakfast nook with her head in her hands.

"Wassup," he spoke, and she jumped.

"He...hey, wassup," she responded nervously.

East gave her a questionable look. "You, aight?"

"Yeah, I'm okay."

"You know I love you right, Emmy."

"Mmmhmm."

"And you can still come to me about anything."

"Mmmhmm." Her phone rang, followed by the doorbell, and he watched her eyes get big. Emersyn got up and darted out of the kitchen.

Fuck she got going on? East thought to himself as he went to answer the door. Checking the peephole, he saw Fabo standing outside, scoping the scene. He was always on guard.

"Come in, nigga," East said, opening the door. Fabo entered the house and looked around as if it was his first time there. "So wassup?"

"Well, we two and a half niggas short," Fabo responded.

"What the hell you mean, two and a half niggas short?"

"Just what I said. Two niggas are dead, and the other nigga is halfway dead." Fabo shrugged like the foolishness that had just come out of his mouth actually made sense.

"Okay, well maybe I'm slow. Tell me how and why we got a half dead nigga." Saying it out loud made East feel as crazy as Fabo sounded when he said it.

"Aight. Picture it! Sicily, 1922."

"Niggaaa, stop playing so fucking much." East had to stop himself from laughing.

"Aight, aight, real shit. I put MoMoney and Roger down cause after I looked at the cameras again, I noticed MoMoney nod towards the back room before the one nigga headed that way. Roger was guilty by association cause him and MoMoney were in the house prior to. Nike is the half dead nigga. I shot him in his dick and in both legs."

"And he's half dead how?"

"Since I felt like he was only halfway listening when I was talking, I took away his most prized possession. You know what kind of hurt, and anguish a nigga gotta go through if he can't use his dick? Pause."

"Nah, man, I don't."

"Me either, but I know I'd rather be dead than to not be able to use mine, so halfway dead he is. Oh, and handicapped. I spared the other niggas at your request. You know, on some team player shit."

Shaking his head, East ran his hand down his face. Fabo was over the top at times, but he always got the job done. "Cool. Did they say if they knew who ran up in the spot?"

"Blaze said he recognized some nigga name Craig or Greg. Wait, nah, it was definitely Craig."

As if on cue, Emersyn walked out into the living room, chewing on her bottom lip. Fabo pulled out his gun and pointed it in her direction.

"Nigga, I'll beat yo motherfuckin' ass," East threatened. "Put that shit away." He smacked Fabo's hand and turned around to see who he was pointing the gun at.

"My bad man," Fabo said, tucking his gun away. "She just came out of nowhere. Shit, ion know her pretty ass."

"Dawg, this my mama crib, don't you think I know the people in here? I be worried about you sometimes, cause ain't no way."

"Eastland, can I talk to you for a minute?" Emersyn asked.

"Hell, no you can't. Where that nigga Craig at?"

"Wait, she know that nigga. Ahh, hell naw."

"Go wait for me outside Fabo."

"Aight, man. Ay, pretty, you need to watch the company you keep," Fabo said to Emersyn before leaving out.

"Did you know that nigga Craig hit my trap?"

"No, I didn't know he went through with it. We've been fighting all week and yesterday we argued about you. He kept saying that I don't respect his hustle because I won't help get him put on. I told him that I didn't know about your business and even if I did, I didn't think you'd wanna work with him anyway. He asked me if I knew where your trap houses were and when I told him I didn't know, this happened." She took off the hoodie she was wearing, showing East the fresh bruises. "I came here because I'm done." Tears fell from Emersyn's eyes. "I'm really done this time."

"Did you overhear him making any plans?"

"Yeah, yesterday morning, he was on the phone with his cousin talking about a move."

"I need a name, Emmy."

"Malcolm. The family calls him, MoMoney."

East was steaming inside. He couldn't believe that Craig had the balls to try him. Then to have an inside man all along was wild. "Where that nigga at now?" East asked through clenched teeth.

"He just text me and said that he's on his way home and I

better be there in fifteen minutes." She held up her phone to show him the text.

"Oh, somebody with the last name Smalls is gonna be there but it won't be you. Gimmie your keys." Digging in her pocket, she took out her house keys and handed them to him. East turned and headed for the door.

"I'm sorry, Eastland. I'm sorry."

"I know," he replied but didn't turn around to see her face. He would deal with his sister and their relationship at another time. He had to tuck his feelings away temporarily. Right now, he had murder on his mind.

Outside, he walked over to Fabo's Range Rover. "Ay, I got something important I need to handle. I'ma text you the address to my sister's crib. You got your kit witchu?"

"My *make a nigga wish I shot em'* kit?"

"Yeah."

"Never leave home without it."

"Here," he gave Fabo Emersyn's keys. "Make that nigga suffer for every bruise he put on my sister's body."

"Oh, most definitely. I got you." They dapped each other up and Fabo pulled off. East could've just put a bullet in Craig's head but sending Fabo was like sending the grim reaper, shit would be ugly.

Chapter 17

"Come on, Tima. I'm trying to be in and out like a robbery." Katori laced up her sneakers and slid her brass knuckles onto her hand.

"I'm ready." Fatima walked out into the living room in sweats, an oversized hood, and a pair of New Balance on her feet.

Katori decided that she wasn't gonna wait until she saw Kita's aunt out in traffic, she was going to deliver the ass whipping right to her. She was thankful for daylight savings time and the time going back because the sun had gone down and it was only six o' clock. Katori planned to move swiftly. Tying her dreads back with two rubber bands, she was ready for action in the same black sweatsuit as Fatima.

"Tae, we'll be back," Katori yelled out to him.

"Aight."

She was glad he didn't come out into the living room asking questions. Although she wouldn't have lied, she felt the less he knew, the better. She and Tima left the house and got into the Uber that was out front waiting on them.

"You know if she home?" Tima asked.

"Unemployed bitches are always home. Besides, it's a Tuesday night so I'm sure she is."

"Alright."

"We gotta make this quick. I gotta be back at the condo for nine."

"Not a curfew," Tima said, cheesing.

"Don't nobody have no damn curfew. I told East I would make him dinner as a thanks for, you know, looking out."

"Mmmhmm, give him a lil dessert, too."

"Shut up," Katori giggled and shoved her. "I'm starting to get a little used to him."

"That's good. You still thinking bout moving?"

"Yeah. I have to. Me and Tae need our own space."

"I get that."

The Uber stopped in front of Kita's aunt's house and there was a crowd of people standing in front of the building. Katori could hear all kinds of shouting going on as she exited the Uber. They knew instantly that there was some shit going on. Going closer to the crowd, Katori was able to see a full-on fight. From the looks of it, there were four girls against three. While two sets of females were in a one on one, the two on one was intense. Noticing Kita's aunt in the squabble, Katori went to step in but was halted by Fatima's voice.

"Ahhh, shit," Fatima let out as she watched East walk over to the crowd. By the look on his face, she could tell he was pissed.

When Katori turned around and saw him, she felt the butterflies and at the same time she was a little scared.

"East…"

"Get yo hardheaded ass in the car, now." He spoke in a low but authoritative tone. She scrunched her face up and went to protest but he stopped her. "Don't play with me, Katori."

Stomping over to his truck, she got inside of the passenger seat, slamming the door behind her. Katori watched as East fussed at Fatima before she stomped over to the car and got in the backseat.

"Bitch, you got me in trouble," she said, laughing.

"Sorry. He ain't nobody damn daddy. Talkin' bout get in the car." Katori sat back in the seat and crossed her arms tightly across her chest.

"You talkin' big shit but you got yo ass in this truck tho." They both cracked up.

Katori stopped laughing when she saw East headed in their direction. "Shut up, he's coming." East swaggered across the street like he owned it. His confidence was on a thousand, boss status times two.

He hopped in the car, turned the radio on, and peeled

out. He had no conversation for either of the women because he was pissed at both, especially Katori. Katori wanted to say something but stayed mute. East seemed to be more upset this time around than he was at the funeral brawl. Figuring that he may want to cancel dinner, she texted Tae to let him know that she was on his way back and if he wanted to come back to the condo with her, he could. She'd told him about the dinner she was making for East, and he'd opted to crash at Fatima's house for the night.

Lil Bro: I'm good. Kita's cousin is coming to scoop me. I'm gonna go chill with her for a little bit and then they gonna drop me back off.

Me: Well, thanks for the heads up.

Lil Bro: My bad. I love you.

Me: Uh, huh. Love you, too.

They arrived at Fatima's house and Katori went to unbuckle her seatbelt.

"Where you going?" East asked her.

"Huh?"

"If you can huh, you can hear. Aren't you supposed to be making me dinner?"

"Yeah, but—."

"Right, I want my food. Goodnight, cuz."

"Goodnight, y'all," Fatima said, getting out of the car.

East pulled off once she walked inside her building.

"Why'd you go out there after I told you I would handle the situation?"

"Cause, I told you I didn't want you to handle it. And I

wanted to deal with that bitch myself."

"And when you pulled up what did you see?"

"Someone clearly got to her before I did." Katori took off the brass knuckles and put them in her pocket.

"Exactly, handled."

"But, how did you know I was gonna…I know Tae didn't rat his own sister out." She went to her text thread with Tae ready to cuss him out.

"Nah, I pulled up over to Tima's house to surprise you with something and you weren't there. He told me y'all went out. It don't take long for my mind to put two and two together. Grab that bag in the back.

She reached in the backseat and picked up the small, black bag. Inside, there was a jewelry box. "What's this?"

"Open it."

She opened the box and there were two sets of keys inside. "Keys? What's going on, Eastland."

"Those are keys for you and Tae, to your new place."

"Wha…what new place? Eastland, what are you talking about?"

The car came to a stop, and he parked. "Come on, witcho dramatic ass." He joked and got out to open the door for her. Katori was in a daze as they walked up to a building similar to his in Westchester, only this one was a few stories higher.

The doorman greeted them, and he guided her to the elevator. East stood behind her as they waited for the elevator in silence. Katori was still tryna wrap her head around him giving her keys and East taking her in. Getting on the elevator, they rode up to the second floor.

"Go head and use your key," he said once they got off the elevator.

"Eastland, stop playing, forreal." She felt tears prickling her eyes.

"Girl, open your door," he pushed.

She stuck her key in the door and turned the lock. East pushed the door open for her and she gasped. The place was beautiful with marble flooring, floor to ceiling windows, and an open floorplan.

"What the hell, why'd you do this?"

"It's my way of apologizing for turning your world upside down. It's also my way of saying, a nigga really wanna fuck witchu, and put you onto some real shit. I don't wanna talk about how we met, I don't wanna hear about morals and all that other shit. Motherfuckers have met in worst scenarios than this. My mama told me when I find the one, I'll know. As crazy as it sounds, I believe the one is your mean ass."

Katori giggled and took two steps so that she was directly in front of him. "I guess mama knows best."

"I know, Ms. Evelyn does."

"From kidnapper to boyfriend, that makes for a good story, huh?"

"Ain't nobody kidnap you, girl. A real hitta snatched yo ass up." East pulled her into him by the small of her back and parted her lips with his tongue. Neither one of them knew what would come of their whirlwind romance, but they knew they would take how they met to the grave.

The End

Did you enjoy the read?
Let us know how much by leaving us a review on Amazon
and Goodreads.

Keep reading for a preview of…

Charge It To The Game

By Nai

PROLOGUE

"This game wasn't meant to be ran by a woman," my father told me as I sat across from him in the visiting room at San Quentin State prison. "It's male dominated just like anything else in this world and that's why you gotta be five steps ahead. You come from my loins, so you already have an advantage. I raised you to be a strong leader and never take no for an answer. Your poise and resilience will play a part in your takeover. I'm passing the baton to you and it's going to fuck up the heads of a lot of people but don't concern yourself with idle chit chat. Keep your womanly mannerisms. Just because you're the boss don't mean that you have to act like a man. Stay the course and do this shit right... the Wright way."

I took in everything he said, soaking the words up like a sponge. I knew what was being asked of me and I had no intentions on letting my father down. I had to act like a woman while thinking like a man. Stepping into the shoes of Curtis "Coolie" Wright wasn't going to be an easy feat, but my daddy didn't raise no hoe. With my Queens by my side, we were sure to shake up the city.

"I hear you, daddy. I'm gonna make sure they never forget your name. It'll be like you never left," I assured him.

"They never forget a Legend, baby girl. You just make sure they know the *new* First Lady at The Table." He reached across the metal table for my hand and squeezed it. It was a sign to let me know that he had to go. Since he started serving his sentence, we had the whole visiting thing down to a science. We never said goodbye because it was too final for me. Instead, he squeezed my hand and I'd say, "until we meet again," and he would nod his head and smile. After doing our ritual, we both stood.

"I love you, daddy."

"I love you too, daughter. Go out there and make me proud."

MAHOGANY

ONE YEAR LATER

I sat at the head of the conference table in one of the office buildings I owned with my best friends, Tiffany and Morae to the left and right of me as we conducted the monthly money meeting for The Table. We each listened as the heads of each borough gave account of what they needed for their re-up as well as handing over our portion of their profit. Everything was going smooth until we got to Briscoe. Briscoe had control of Brooklyn. His cocky ass couldn't take the fact that *I* now ran the entire operation. It didn't help that we were ex-lovers. Since I'd been put in position, he made sure to never miss an opportunity to act like a dickhead.

"This nigga," Tiffany whispered as we watched Briscoe play on his phone as if he didn't know it was his time to report. "Ay, Briscoe, I don't know if you think the concept no longer applies to you, but time is money. And right now, you wasting it. Report, nigga," she pushed.

"Oh, it's my turn?" He played dumb. Reaching down, he picked up an MCM book bag off the floor and sat it on the table. "That's seventy bands." Morae got up and snatched the bag off the table before proceeding to the money room to count it. Like Tiffany, she was tired of his bullshit too.

Over his shenanigans and blatant disrespect, I leaned forward and folded one black, gel- manicured hand over the other before speaking. "You've wasted five minutes of my time that I can never get back. I'm gonna need you to go ahead and add five thousand to your monthly payout. That's a stack for each minute wasted." The smirk he had on his face was now gone.

"Oh, you fining niggas now over bullshit? Get the fuck outta here Mahogany. The way I'm out here bringing in money and you tryna *lil boy* me?" He stood in a threatening manner and from the corner of my eye, I could see Tiffany place her gun on the table.

"All of this huffing and puffing over five G'z, Briscoe? Damn, I'm disappointed in you, baby. I suggest you pipe the fuck down though; you know how Tiff gets when she feels I'm being disrespected." Slowly, he sat down, and I knew by the slits in his eyes he was embarrassed and pissed about it. I gave not one fuck because he had brought it on himself. "Trick, you're up."

I listened as Trick, who sat to the left of Briscoe, gave his report while Briscoe stared a hole in the side of my face.

From day one, he didn't respect my position. He thought that by my father treating him like a son when we were together, he was being groomed to be next in line. He was sadly mistaken because I always knew the operation would be handed over to me if something happened to my dad. It got under his skin that he had to answer to me, a woman. I held the power for him to keep getting money in the city.

"Aight, meeting adjourned," Morae spoke after reentering the room. "Same time next month fellas. If for any reason you need to re-up earlier than your scheduled time, you know where to find me." With no further words spoken, everyone got up to make their exit. As usual, once everyone cleared out, the ladies and I debriefed. I didn't let Briscoe get by me though.

"Aye Briscoe," I called out to the angry man, "you're forgetting something." Tiffany smirked when he turned around. Digging in his pocket, he counted out fifty $100 bills and placed the blue faces on the table. I watched as he ran his tongue over his teeth before pushing the money towards me. I knew he wanted to say something but opted out of it. "Thank you, love." He nodded his head and walked out. Nobody's ever always happy with the boss.

"You need to let his ass go. That nigga so envious of you, it don't even make no sense," Morae said as we debriefed and put away the monthly take.

"I agree with Mo. He wants yo' position bad," Tiffany added. I knew they were right, but the only thing stopping me from cutting Briscoe off was the fact that he did bring in money--lots of it. Although he acted like a bitch behind me being over him, he hadn't snaked me on the business side. I couldn't say that I knew how long it would last though.

"I hear what y'all saying and trust me when I say I'm keeping an eye on him. Briscoe may envy me, but he knows betta than to cross me. He loves his family too much." In the Wright organization, we were big on loyalty and didn't allow second chances when it came down to it. You crossed us, we let everyone close to you feel it and leave you alive just so you could live with the fact that you were the reason for their demise.

"Look, I'll never tell you how to handle business, but I'm telling you the longer you let that nigga live with that malice in his heart, that shit is just going to fester. And that's going to be bad for business," Morae spoke again.

I looked over at her and smirked. "You just want to kill him, don't you?"

"Oh, please, please, please." She had her hands up in a praying motion while she bat her eyes. "I promise not to make it messy."

"Our friend is really looney," Tiffany joked, walking out of the vault while I shook my head and followed.

"Nuts I tell you." I laughed and Mo rolled her eyes at the both of us.

"Y'all never let me have no fun, it's cool though. And how

you gon' call me looney when you practically live at the shooting range?" She closed the door behind us and locked it and I looked over at Tiff.

"Hey, I have my thing and you have yours." Tiffany shrugged her shoulders and smirked. I loved my girls. Tiffany was my God sister and we'd known Morae since we were ten. Still in our twenties, we had made a name for ourselves in the game. Morae, Tiffany, and I were three different women that bought different skillsets and personalities to The Table which enabled our business to be such a success.

Tiffany was my beautiful, head of security. With a pretty face, stacked body, and a keen sense of style, one would never peg her as anyone's protector. What people didn't know was that Tiffany was just as deadly if not deadlier than most of the killers I knew. Growing up a military kid, Tiff knew her way around guns. It wasn't uncommon for her to have us at the gun range at any given time, testing out some new shit.

Morae was head lieutenant. She ran all of our spots and ran them with an iron fist. Cold as a motherfucka too. While each borough had its HNIC, such as the guys that were gathered tonight, before anything got to my ears, it went through Mo first. She was my eyes and ears on the ground. Couldn't nobody get to me until they went through her. And even then, Mo had the answers because she knew how I was going to step at all times. A petite thing standing at 5'5, Mo had the shape of an athlete.

She stayed in the gym, toning, but maintained her feminine energy. It was likely why she attracted both women and men but preferred to play on the same team. I pondered everyday why she chose to lick cat as opposed to having a hard dick. To each's own though. More than the skillsets they brought to The Table, I knew for a fact that my bitches were some riders. They would go to war with an army behind me and I knew I didn't have to question the love or loyalty they had for me.

The game was treacherous, and in order to survive in it, you had to have people who were gonna step behind you, no questions asked. I had that times two, well three if you included my father. Shit, even behind the wall, if Coolie wanted you touched, you got touched. Those bars didn't mean shit. As for me, I was the team's all-around player, keeping things running like a well-oiled machine in the background.

To the world, I was Mahogany Wright, the woman behind the infamous "Elite Palace." A popular gentlemen's club in Westchester, NY. I had the baddest bitches, and the niggas came from far and wide to be a part of the "Elite Experience." There was something for everybody at Elite, though. We didn't just cater to the men.

While I had a host of beautiful women who worked in my club, my premiere dancers made it so that it was the talk of the city. Cherokee, Bad Ass Bri, Kat, and Paris were handpicked by me and Morae. We'd done a good job because not only did they make the niggas spend bands, but they were also trained to kill any motherfucka that was a threat. I ran my club just as I'd run The Table in many ways, with a strict no bullshit policy. I didn't allow drugs in my establishment unless I was the one supplying them, and it was never anything hard. I supplied edibles and free hookah. If you wanted a different high, you could purchase any exotic weed of your choosing or X.

"Are you going into the club tonight?" Mo asked as we walked to our cars. Daylight savings had rolled around, and it was darker than usual for it to only be eight o'clock.

"Not tonight. I promised Beautii I'd be home after this meeting. She wants me to take her out to dinner, said she needs to talk to me."

"If Beautii don't go head," Tiffany laughed. "My girl wanna talk over dinner. I swear she is you all day." It was true, my nine-year-old daughter was a mini me. She had my face and my mannerisms down to a T.

"Yeah, that's my baby so you know I gotta make it happen. What y'all getting into?" Using my remote starter to start my Porsche Cayenne Coupe, I walked around the driver's side to get in.

"After I make sure you get home, I'm gonna take it in for the night. I don't feel like being around a crowd and you know tomorrow is brunch with my dad. I gotta be up and before time."

"And alert," I reminded Tiffany.

"As fuck. You know he don't give a bitch a break. What

about you, Mo?" Tiffany asked Morae whose head was in her phone. "Mo!" Tiff yelled out to get her attention.

Mo's eyes shot up and annoyance was written all over her face. "You ain't have to do all that. And yeah, I'm gonna swing by the club a little later to see Paris."

I smirked, opening my door to put my purse inside. "You are smitten by that girl."

"I ain't smitten by nobody. I do fuck with her heavy though," she called herself correcting me.

"Girl, that is just the hood definition of smitten." We all shared a laugh, and she waved me off.

"I'll hit the chat once I make it to the club," she said and went to hop in her car. Beeping the horn twice once she started it up, she drove off into the night.

I didn't mind Mo dating one of my dancers because we had long ago set boundaries. She knew she couldn't hoard Paris when she was on the clock and there was no PDA on the floor. I was big on not mixing business with pleasure and Mo respected that. I also lead by example which was why I made sure to separate how I felt about Briscoe from the business.

"You ready?" Tiffany nodded towards me.

"Yeah." I climbed into my car and connected to my Blue-tooth to call Beautii.

"Hey, mommy," she answered, not letting the call ring fully.

"Hey, sugar, were you waiting by the phone?"

"Yep. Are you on your way home?"

I smiled and shook my head. "**I am, so you can start getting dressed. Where's Gran?**" I asked about my mother.

"**In the kitchen, reading.**"

"**Okay, I'll see you in a minute. Be dressed when I come through the door, Beautii.**"

"**I will. Love you, mommy.**"

"**I love you too, my girl.**" Ending the call just as Tiff pulled up next to me, I rolled down my window.

"You down to put some speed on yo' baby tonight?" She was referring to my car. We had pulled up to the meeting in the same car and cracked up at the coincidence.

"Not tonight, Tiff. Let's just get home."

"Ahh, okay. I knew you was scared I was gon' dust yo' ass. Go head and pull out, I'm right behind you."

I smirked and gave her the finger. Truth was, I didn't feel like racing because the girls' comments were on my mind. Briscoe was showing his ass and the last thing I was gonna tolerate was him thinking he was above The Table. I'd hate to have to put my daughter's father under it.

Available Now On Amazon

OTHER BOOKS BY

URBAN AINT DEAD

Tales 4rm Da Dale

The Hottest Summer Ever

By **Elijah R. Freeman**

Despite The Odds

By **Juhnell Morgan**

Good Girl Gone Rogue

By **Manny Black**

Hittaz 1, 2 & 3

Coldhearted

By **Lou Garden Price, Sr.**

A Summer To Remember With My Hitta

Charge It To The Game 1 & 2

By **Nai**

A Setup For Revenge

By **Ashley Williams**

Ridin' For You

By **Telia Teanna**

The State's Witness 1 & 2

By **Kyiris Ashley**

Stuck In The Trenches 1 & 2

By **Huff Tha Great**

The Swipe

By **Toōla**

Charge It To The Game 3
By **Nai**

The Swipe 2
By **Toōla**

BOOKS BY

URBAN AINT DEAD's C.E.O

<u>Elijah R. Freeman</u>

Triggadale 1, 2 & 3

Tales 4rm Da Dale

The Hottest Summer Ever

Murda Was The Case 1, 2 & 3

Follow
Elijah R. Freeman
On Social Media

FB: Elijah R. Freeman

IG: @the_future_of_urban_fiction